WHAT WE DO *for Love*

***What We Do for Love* by Anne Pfeffer**

First Edition, May 2019

Bold Print Press
Los Angeles, CA

www.annepfeffer.com

ISBN: 978-1-7338220-0-8 (print), 978-1-7338220-1-5 (epub)

Proofreading: Shayla Raquel, ShaylaRaquel.com
Cover Design: James, GoOnWrite.com
Interior Formatting: Melinda Martin, MartinPublishingServices.com

WHAT WE DO *for Love*

A Novel

ANNE PFEFFER

Other works by Anne Pfeffer

Any Other Night

The Wedding Cake Girl

Girls Love Travis Walker

Just Pru

To Laura,
best kid in the universe

Chapter 1

Funny how one's life can make a U-turn.

My life made two. In a single day.

I started that day as a mere potter—yes, a person who handmakes vases and dinner plates for a living—wearing borrowed clothes and driving to the most important interview of my life. A few hours later came U-turn number one: the board of directors of CCMLA, the Contemporary Crafts Museum of Los Angeles, offered me a place in their upcoming show!

In an instant, I had become an artist. I pondered this fact wonderingly as I drove home that afternoon. I was to provide them with a brand-new, never-before-seen mural in ceramics, an installation piece. My wall would be located at the entrance to the exhibit, the first thing you saw as you walked in. This was my chance, an incredible opportunity.

I was an artist!

It didn't bother me that desperation clearly underlay the board's decision. All the better when I saved the day with a great contribution to their show.

I hoped.

Flushed with success, I revved my ancient Toyota, Bernice, up to twenty-two miles per hour. We practically skipped over the potholes as we barreled our way up the Trail of Terror. This was the name my son Justin had given the rutted, one-lane road that wound its way up the side of Laurel Canyon to our house.

Of course, I was a fill-in, hired at the last minute. I'd gotten this job when Miriam Fletcher, a customer of mine who happened to be on the museum board, moaned to me that an artist had dropped out of a show scheduled to open in six weeks. "We're in such a pickle! We don't know what to do!" Though her crepey neck revealed a senior citizen, Miriam otherwise projected youth, running long acrylic nails through her cropped, bleached, and spiked hair, her copper earrings swinging.

My cue to pipe up. "I'm sure I could help you."

Miriam trained her eyes upon me. She had recently ordered customized handmade pieces from me to give to her granddaughters—a miniature tea set for the youngest and a statuette of a mermaid for her older sister.

"You do such beautiful ceramics work, Nicole."

"What you've seen is my commercial work, which I do through my business Clayworks. I create as an artist under my own name." That is, I *hoped* to create as an artist under my own name, if I could ever get the proper start.

And now I had. I could hardly wait to tell my son the news. After sixteen years of single motherhood and hard work, struggling to support myself and Justin, I couldn't blow this chance. And yet, I'd never done anything like this before.

A twelve-by-nine-foot mural. In just six weeks.

You can do this, I told myself. I had to. Letting the museum—and myself—down was unthinkable.

I could practically hear the snap-crackle-pop of my nerves.

I pulled into what we called the car park, an open space situated beside the house at the top of the Trail of Terror, big enough to park a half dozen cars. Justin's Ford Focus wasn't there.

When he got home from school, which should be any minute, we would raise a toast, our champagne glasses filled with sparkling apple cider.

The day was unseasonably hot, and I was boiling in Bernice, her air conditioner long dead. Thank heavens my hair had stayed up all day in the deliberately loose knot that I'd coaxed it into this morning, with pretty little bits of hair hanging down around my face. A chignon, according to the YouTube tutorial. One more degree of humidity and my whole head would have coiled itself into a giant Brillo pad right there before the entire board of directors.

And thank goodness I'd been able to borrow my sister's striking red-and-orange color-blocked linen dress, which had given me just the boost of artist/business woman confidence that I'd needed. Now though, its linen skirt was hopelessly creased and hiking up around my hips. I bounded out of the car and proceeded along the circuitous route that we all used to enter the house, going through the rickety side gate and past what was technically our front door, which no one ever opened. Instead, I followed the path that ran alongside the house toward the yard and pool, giving a glance to my irises and roses, which grew under our bedroom windows.

The white, yellow, and purple irises stood tall and elegant, but it was the roses I really loved—the fluttery, homegrown variety that came in every color of the sunrise. I would have to harvest some for tonight's dinner table.

As I reached the yard, I stepped from the cool shade of the side path into direct, hot sunshine. The sliver of Los Angeles ahead of me that appeared on clear days like this one, the perfume of herbs and blooming plants, the swimming pool that shimmered invitingly—except for my college years, this had been home all my life. Along with my sister Caroline, I'd inherited the small, dilapidated house on its magnificent parcel of land in the Hollywood Hills. At today's prices, neither of us could have ever afforded to buy it.

Entering the house as always through the French doors off the living room, I waltzed into my bedroom. It was the beginning of a new era. Soon, there would be no more making pottery on consignment. No more sets of dinnerware for twelve.

I shouldn't get ahead of myself. Of course, I would continue to operate Clayworks. Those dinner sets paid the bills after all. Still, though, there was now a chance I could taper off the business over time, if I could sell some of my more creative pieces. Imagine me, finally, at age thirty-eight, beginning to show in museums and galleries.

I changed into my regular daywear—a sleeveless cotton blouse, long flowy skirt in the coolest featherlight cotton, and Teva sandals.

My old friend Mike Sawyer would be over to eat with Justin and me as he did most weeks, once or twice. Maybe I'd give them both my wonderful news at the same time.

No, I couldn't wait that long to spread the news. I knew I would tell Justin the minute he walked in.

Hearing the muffled noise of a door opening, I sprinted to the kitchen, where my son, home at last, would for sure want to hear all about it.

I stopped short when I saw that Justin was not alone.

Chapter 2

For the first time ever, my sixteen-year-old son had brought home a girl. The teenagers stood side by side in my kitchen, inches apart yet separate, like strangers on a bus.

The girl wore neatly pressed jeans and a top that left her arms and shoulders bare. Free of makeup, she was as young and fresh and lovely as a rosebud from my garden.

Justin was long, lean, and blond, like his father, my ex. He wore his hair spiky on top and shaved on one side, a pair of second-hand army boots on his feet. His jeans were faded from hundreds of washings and bore holes that showed glimpses of his knees. No tattoos yet, but he was already working me over on that one.

Despite his coolness and classic good looks, I can't say I'd seen him give much attention to the opposite sex up to now. I'd loved having over the many male friends he'd brought home in the past, with their careless thumps and shouts and their basketballs, Slip 'N Slides, guitars, and mixtapes.

But a girl! Pushing her dark, heavy curls back behind her shoulders, she looked around her, uncertain, rubbing the toe of her sneaker against her ankle.

Justin, too, had this lost look about him, as if he were trying to navigate an unknown landscape. Usually the screen door banged to announce his arrival, followed by the thump of his backpack as it hit the floor. Today, he had entered quietly and hung it on a wall hook.

Of course, I didn't know at the time that my life was careening straight toward U-turn number two.

Justin inclined his head in the girl's direction. "Mom, this is Daniela."

"Welcome!" I smiled and stuck out my hand.

After a second's hesitation, Daniela managed to extend her own hand and give me a small smile. "It's so nice to meet you, Ms. Adams."

"Nicole," I said automatically.

"Nicole." Her glance moved across our kitchen island to the large living room sofa, covered with a colorful throw, the brass teapot on the coffee table, and sun shining through the French doors that led to the patio outside. Natural light brightened the dark hardwood floors and ceiling beams. I thought the place looked pleasant and welcoming, despite the missing door handle and the crack on the top of the coffee table.

Spotting a peach-colored ceramic vase, one of my own pieces, filled with white hydrangeas from the garden, Daniela caught her breath, smiled, and reached out a finger to touch it. "Your house is so pretty!"

No jaded LA teenager here. Her obvious pleasure in my home charmed me, yet when she raised her dark, expressive eyes to meet mine, I was shocked to see the pain in them. Shaken, I dropped my own eyes, feeling almost as if I'd seen something I wasn't supposed to.

I felt that familiar and absurd need I got around Justin and his friends to tackle them to the ground, interrogate them, and find out everything about them. Put them in a headlock, if necessary, to pry their adolescent secrets out of them.

What were their guilty pleasures? What kinds of people did they choose to be around? Did they believe in a higher power, and if so, was it a conscious being?

And why was this girl in pain? I didn't ask those questions, of course. I'd learned that personal information from a teenager was like rain in the desert. You waited for it, sometimes for months, and viewed every drop as a gift.

In the face of her distress, I would hold off until the right moment to share my incredible news.

Justin began serving drinks, taking out glasses and bottles of juice.

"So, Daniela, are you also a junior at Laurelmont?"

"I am. I just started there this year, in September."

My son pulled an old-fashioned tray of ice cubes from our antiquated freezer and broke some out into a glass. As he handed it to her, a complex look—apprehension, maybe, mingled with urgency—passed between them, causing a tiny crack to appear on the smooth surface of my mind. I was too preoccupied to focus on it.

"Where did you move from?"

"Las Vegas." She paused, then went on. "My mom got a nursing job here in LA."

"Your mom's a nurse?"

"Yeah. An obstetrical nurse." For just a moment, pride lit up Daniela's face.

"And your dad?"

The pride ebbed away. "Oh, he's in . . . consulting."

"Daniela's mom is a *bad ass*," Justin cut in, nodding his encouragement to the girl. "She delivered a baby once in the parking lot of Big Buys in Vegas. It was on the news! And she got an award from her hospital."

"She must be really proud! I'm surprised she wanted to leave."

"The ob/gyn she liked working with left," Daniela said. "Dr. Azirian."

I nodded.

"She invented a machine," the girl went on, "the doctor, I mean. All the hospitals started buying it, and she found out she could make more money that way than delivering babies."

"Really!" I glanced at my watch, sorry to interrupt what had turned into an interesting conversation. "I've got to get some dinner on the table. Would you like to join us, Daniela?"

"Yes, please!"

Justin cleared his throat. "And, well . . ." He stopped, glancing at me and Daniela, then said in a rush, "Maybe she could stay here overnight too."

"Overnight!" Caught by surprise, I took a deep breath. "You have school tomorrow."

"She needs a place to stay." Justin's eyes met mine in a direct plea.

"What about *her home*?" I threw a questioning look to Daniela, who seemed to shrink inside, becoming even smaller than she already was. "Honey, where are your parents?" I asked her.

"Umm." Daniela seemed to have gone mute.

"They threw her out," Justin interjected, scowling.

The amazing badass baby nurse had thrown her kid out of the house? No wonder Daniela was so unhappy. And the dad? Where was he in all this?

"Your parents told you not to come home?"

"Uh-huh." She pressed her lips tightly together.

"Do they know you're here?"

"No."

I nodded slowly, only half believing the story. Not because she seemed to be lying, but because I couldn't fathom a parent doing such a thing.

Justin leaned toward me over the island, his hands braced against the worn tiles. "It's cool, Mom. She can have my bed, and I'll sleep in the living room."

Trust me, he was saying. His eyes shone with sincerity. I'd always given him the benefit of the doubt when he made me a promise, and he had never before abused the privilege.

The girl must be another one of Justin's strays. He'd brought them home all his life—abandoned dogs and cats, a couple of neighbor kids whose mom worked late—not to mention members of his regular circle of friends, who, at various times for various reasons, had stayed with us. Justin brought them all here, confident they would be housed, fed, and entertained.

A movement caught my eye. Had I seen that right? Yes, for a second, Justin had rested his eyes on the girl's shoulder, where the thin black edge of her tank top slipped down, revealing a fashionably bright-orange bra strap. She had what my son and his friends referred to as a "slammin' body," slender in those crisp jeans and black tank.

My internal Mother's Early Warning System began to beep. *Caution. Caution. Adult supervision advised.* At this age, boys were approaching their sexual peak. They were like roosters, programmed to populate the earth.

Of course he's thinking about sex, I reminded myself. *He's sixteen.* Time was moving on. It was just my hopeful-but-deluded mother's heart that preferred to think of him as an eight-year-old.

Better that than admit to myself that he was likely following the same path I'd taken as a teen. At his age, I suddenly recalled, I was fully versed in the arts of first and second base. The badge of virginity I'd kept only until my freshman year of college, when I gave it up to a guy in my study group.

The kids were looking at me, waiting for an answer.

"Let me speak with your parents, Daniela," I said. "Maybe we can work something out. Or at least, they'll know where you are."

Justin nodded meekly, while Daniela seemed to almost collapse with relief to have an adult helping her. "Thank you," she whispered. She pushed a button on her cell phone and handed it to me. "This is my mom's cell."

"What's her name?"

"Viviana . . . Viviana Harris."

I heard a recorded female voice with an accent saying to leave a message.

"Hello, Viviana. This is Nicole Adams. Your daughter Daniela is a friend of my son's. She's at my home right now, and I wanted to speak to you if I may. Please call me." I left my phone number.

Surely Daniela's parents would come for her. They would be frantic soon, if they really didn't know where she was. "So," I said brightly, "we'll discuss all this when they call back."

"They won't," Justin predicted, hunched over, his elbows on the island.

How could he possibly know that? Before I could ask, he spoke up again. "All right! We're going to my room to do homework."

What? I was so not prepared for all this. What kind of relationship did he have with this girl?

I found myself yelling to them as they headed off, "Keep the door open, okay?"

Chapter 3

Forget sparkling apple cider. I spent the next hour chopping up cucumbers and tomatoes that I'd purchased in large boxes from Big Buys. I'd planned to use them in recipes throughout the week. But now, I found them to be a handy excuse to lurk in the kitchen, by all appearances preparing a salad, yet in fact poised to swoop in and bust these kids, should they stray from their formulas and flash cards.

It didn't help that Justin looked so much like Brady, his gorgeous father. They both had that perfect straight nose, hazel eyes that separated into blue, green, and gray pixels in certain kinds of light, and a smile so endearing that you couldn't help but love them.

Until, as in Brady's case, you got to know his true reptilian self.

Justin and his dad were so alike from the outside and yet, thank goodness, so different as humans. At least, I'd always told myself that.

Although my son was stubborn and difficult sometimes (who wasn't?), he had a creative spirit, a good heart, and a goofy sense of humor that made me laugh. His father had been a different story, with his inexplicable rages, coldness, and profound sense of entitlement. I hadn't seen Brady since Justin was a baby. I'd heard he'd gone to Oahu, where he now reportedly owned a pineapple farm. Justin had no memory of him, obviously, and never spoke of him.

As I cut and diced and chopped, I reminded myself that Mike was coming by to have dinner and leave his dogs. They'd be with us for just a few nights while their human counterpart was on location in Dallas.

I would tell Mike about all of today's events—the wonderful new career opportunity that had taken an unexpected back seat to the arrival of a mysterious homeless girl. Par for the course, I thought, my mood both accepting and annoyed. The job of motherhood trumped all others.

Mike would listen to me. He would care. Hard to believe that this man, my true-blue platonic friend for twenty years, was once my lover for almost four months. This was back when we were too young to know better.

During that time, I had loved him in the way that only the really young can, with an all-consuming passion. I was eighteen, and it was the first time I'd ever felt that way about a boy. I quivered at the sight of him, counted the minutes between our times together, and revisited every word we spoke over and over again in my head. The fact that we were friends today testified to how sincerely sorry Mike had been for being young and full of adventure and not ready to settle down, and also to his unique brand of bulldog perseverance. He'd become a trusted friend.

Without benefits.

Those, he got elsewhere.

Losing him at eighteen had broken my heart for a time. But far worse had been my disastrous marriage, which had finished me off, chewing me up and spitting me out in small pieces.

"You're cold and unresponsive," Brady started telling me after he'd lost interest in me. "It makes you less and less attractive to me."

Stricken, I would say, "I'm trying!" He'd been so wonderful in the beginning. But how could I feel sexy in bed when he started describing me as "big" and "broad across the beam"? How could I feel relaxed and confident when he called my clothes frumpy and my cooking bland?

I became unsure of myself, calling my best girlfriend Jamie all the time for advice, since it seemed like everything I did annoyed him. If I were playing my music when he got home, he would stalk over and turn it off. He ridiculed a series of paintings I'd done until I eventually took them down off the wall.

Almost no one in my life had liked Brady.

"He's not a very loving person," my sister had said.

"He's a fuckwit. Sorry." That, from Jamie.

Mike had simply begged me not to marry Brady. When I did it anyway, he'd decamped to South Africa and stayed away for two years, building homes and teaching English.

By now, it was 6:15, and my listening in on the kids had revealed nothing beyond some talk of steam engines and the Industrial Revolution. I strolled down the hall and knocked on Justin's doorframe. They were both seated on the bed, but cross-legged, a respectable distance apart, their laptops and textbooks spread out in a convincingly authentic way.

"Mike'll be here any minute," I told Justin. "Dinner's almost ready. Would you kids help me a little before we eat?"

"Of course!" Daniela jumped to her feet.

A minute later, I was handing her placemats and leading her out the French doors, my hands full of plates and silverware. It was a balmy spring night, perfect for eating outside.

"Hope the road coming up here didn't bother you," I said. It was a full mile up the Trail of Terror from Laurel Canyon Boulevard to our house. Unlit at night, it was memorable for the way the cliff soared straight up on one side of it and plunged straight down on the other.

"It was a little scary, but with Justin driving, I didn't mind it so much."

"Good!" Those winding paths could come as a shock to the canyon's newcomers, especially the first time they tried them.

Daniela's dark curls swung forward as she leaned over to help set our battered picnic table for dinner. It stood in the yard under the shade of some trees. "I like your plates," she said, taking one and holding it up to the light. They were a soft yellow with an abstract pattern around the rim. "They're different."

"I made them, right here at home in my studio. That's what I do." And suddenly, it all came rushing out. "The thing is, though, I've always wanted to do more. Be an actual artist. And I just found out today . . . I'm going to have a piece in a museum show!"

Daniela's face lit up to an extent that satisfied even me. She pumped me with questions: What kind of piece was it? What would it look like? What would serve as its inspiration?

I'd never spoken to anyone about my art in that kind of detail. I found myself blathering on about my most closely held dream to this stranger, this girl I'd met two hours ago.

"I'm thinking of a mural in ceramic tiles. But I don't know exactly what I'm going to do yet." I hesitated. "The theme of the show is *How We Live*."

Daniela's forehead crinkled. "*How We Live?* That's pretty . . . general, I guess."

"Yeah. I can go in a lot of different directions with it." I wasn't sure if it was a blessing or a curse.

We were interrupted by a car horn from the driveway, along with the barking of dogs.

"Down, beasts!" Mike shouted as he followed his two large canines in through the side gate. Sweet, gentle Midge and Margo, named after Mike's sisters, were mutts he had rescued from shelters. They bounded forward, tongues lolling, ears flapping, ready for a party. Justin and Daniela bent over the dogs, scratching their heads and talking to them.

Mike approached me with a wine bottle and a small, wrapped box. "Just a token," he said, "for taking care of the fleabags." He set the gifts onto the picnic table and swept me up in a hug that lifted my feet from the ground, while he smooched my cheek with gusto. "How's my favorite girl?"

"You're such a flirt." I couldn't help feeling a little tingle, even though it didn't mean anything. My friends and I were all touchy-feely types.

He set me down. His gap-toothed smile reminded me of the kid I'd known all those years ago, instead of the forty-year-old man he was now. Broad shouldered and solidly built, he had prematurely gray hair and a keen intelligence that shone through his eyes and smile.

Mike was easy to look at, I'd always thought, but I was glad I'd decided to place him, and all men, forever in the friend zone. After my flameouts with him and Brady, followed by ten years of dating hell, I'd sworn off love and sex forever.

Just as some people swear off carbohydrates, I had come to realize that these things weren't good for my system.

Chapter 4

As darkness fell, my little collection of outdoor lights blinked on, a mixture of paper lanterns and tiny white Christmas lights triggered by an automatic timer. They cast a soft circle that illuminated the table under the trees, with its roses and ceramic pottery, and left the rest of the yard dark. Daniela clapped her hands at the sight.

I loved that, here in the heart of a seething urban mass of over thirteen million people, it was possible to live in this calm, secluded grove. We sat down to dinner.

"Whoa! Fiber, anyone?" Justin did an elaborate comic double take at the massive bowl of cucumbers and tomatoes I'd brought out, enough to feed a stadium.

We grazed on the enormous salad. We ate lasagna with garlic bread and sipped Mike's wine.

"So, they gonna blow you up this time?" Justin was speaking to Mike,

"All I know for sure is I have to crash a race car at a hundred miles per hour. They'll probably at least set me on fire." He tossed a piece of cherry tomato into the air and caught it in his mouth. Mike worked as a stuntman in big action pictures where he routinely plunged through plate-glass windows, fell from helicopters, and fought hand-to-hand battles with knives and clubs.

Justin and his friends worshiped him.

We continued our meal, Daniela eating quietly while Justin seemed to have run out of steam, withdrawing silently into himself. Mike turned to me. "So what's up with you?"

Finally! "I'm going to be in a museum show!" I told them everything, ending with, "And you guys can all come to the opening. You too, Daniela!"

Mike enveloped me in another hug that smelled of pine and peppermint, his stubbly cheek scratching mine. "You deserve this."

"Awesome, Mom," Justin announced, beaming at me. "See, Daniela, *my* mom's kinda badass too!"

His comment warmed my heart. "I won't be delivering any babies soon, but thank you."

"What're you gonna make?" Mike asked.

Happy to be there with my two favorite guys in the whole world, along with this new girl who seemed so sweet and interested, I sat with them under the twinkle lights brainstorming ideas for my mural. It was one of those gorgeous California evenings when the air smells of jasmine and orange blossoms and touches your skin so gently, and you can't believe you're lucky enough to live in such a great place with such terrific friends.

We were still talking about it as Mike helped us clear and wash the dishes, then brought in from his Jeep a bag of kibble and a cooler of frozen raw meat, specially formulized for dogs. He began his lecture about the crucial kibble-to-meat ratio.

"I know, I know!" I told him, laughing and waving him away. "I've done this before."

"Gotta be sure," he told me with a grave expression. "This new formula keeps 'em lean and mean."

"I see that."

We looked down at Margo, who lay on her back whimpering for a belly rub.

"Pansy," Mike grumbled, leaning down to scratch her fur, while her hind leg kicked uncontrollably.

I watched them fondly as Margo leaped to lick Mike's face.

"How's Caroline doing?" he asked after a minute. My sister had split from her husband Grant two weeks ago, and the shock waves were still reverberating through our inner circle of friends. To those of us who knew them, Grant and Caroline were a given in the universe, like the tides or the moon. I didn't even know who my sister was without him.

"About as well as you'd imagine," I said. "She's coming over tomorrow morning."

"Say hi for me."

"I will. Have a good trip," I said.

He kissed the top of my head, wrestled briefly with Justin and the dogs, bid a polite goodbye to Daniela, and left. The kitchen seemed empty without his broad shoulders in the middle of things.

By nine o'clock, Daniela's parents still hadn't called back.

Justin gave me a pointed look. *Told you so.*

Shocked by the apparent indifference of these people, I asked, "How do they know you're safe? You could be camping under the freeway right now."

Daniela's voice quavered. "I'm sure they think I'm fine." The sadness in her voice tore me up.

"They've got to be worried." The tiny crack in my mind had widened just a bit, and a tremor of . . . something . . . ran through me—a premonition, maybe? Or maybe just nerves. "Even if you've had a disagreement, they still love you. They're your parents."

"They're not worried."

I tried to keep my tone brisk and matter-of-fact. "If that's the case, then of course you must stay tonight."

"Thank you," Daniela whispered. At my request, she dialed her phone again and handed it to me. I left another message.

"Hello, Viviana. This is Nicole again. Since I haven't been able to reach you, Daniela will stay the night here, in a separate room from my son. I'll make sure she gets to school on time tomorrow. Please feel free to call me." I left my phone number again, feeling my temper rise as I thought of what these parents had done tonight.

"So," I said, "let's get ready for bed!" I kept my voice bright and chipper. "Justin, will you move your sheets out onto the sofa? I'll put some fresh ones on your bed for Daniela."

By comparison to Justin's male friends, whose presence resounded through the house like a herd of elephants, Daniela was almost ghostlike, blending into the background and whispery quiet. And eager to please.

"Let me put the sheets on," she said. "You shouldn't have to do that."

"All right, thanks." I found her an unused toothbrush and an old T-shirt of mine to sleep in. "And here's a clean towel."

Justin's small bedroom still had its blue plaid wallpaper. The bedspread had borne pictures of teddy bears until he revolted in his freshman year of high school, requesting a plain blue comforter. Justin's stuff filled every corner and covered every surface: music posters, two guitars and a drum, his bicycle, a debate trophy, comic books, and books with art or math and logic puzzles.

"Thank you again." Daniela drooped as she sat down on the bed.

"Are you all right, honey?" I sat down next to her. "Do you want to tell me a little more about what's going on?"

The two dogs galumphed into the room just as Justin's tall, lean frame appeared in the doorway, dressed in the sweatpants and T-shirt he usually wore to bed. Midge and Margo rushed the twin bed, trying to climb aboard, but I gently pushed them down onto the rug. I put my arm around Daniela as she shuddered and the tears started to fall. She gripped her hands together tightly. "I did something . . . that my parents didn't like. My dad especially."

Justin fastened his gaze on her as she spoke. His bleak eyes reminded me of the time he'd found a dead baby rabbit in the swimming pool. My throat suddenly felt dry, and a chill ran over me despite the balmy evening air.

"My mom would forgive me, but Dad won't let me live at home anymore."

"I'm sure he'll reconsider. You know, once he cools off." What could this girl have done? Totaled the family car? Burned down the house?

Could she be . . . ?

No way. I wouldn't permit myself to have the thought. *She's only sixteen.*

Justin spoke up, his voice harsh in the silence. "We have to tell her, Daniela."

Up until now, I'd thought, or kidded myself, that Justin was only helping a girl with a problem. Now, the fear arose that it might be Justin's problem too.

I held my breath.

"Daniela's pregnant," Justin said. "And I'm the father."

Chapter 5

That was U-turn number two, and on the very day that I'd gotten some of the best news of my life. It was as if someone up there thought I needed to be taken down a peg.

I was silent in the face of Justin's confession. The little boy I knew inside and out had, with a single sentence, become a stranger.

Until this moment, I would have told you he was a virgin, not interested in girls yet, inexperienced in dealing with the opposite sex. I would have said that we were close, that he told me the important things, that I knew the terrain of his mind and his life.

Now, he didn't even look the same to me. When had the dark shadow across his chin become so prominent? The tired slump of his shoulders was not that of a boy, but rather of the man he was about to become.

And what kind of man was that? A man like his father, who'd been so charming and kind, a man whose inner darkness only showed itself later?

This person was not the timid child who had held my hand crossing the street and crawled into my bed when an owl hooted in the canyon. This was a young man who had lied to me, probably repeatedly, about where he was and what he was doing. A man who had experienced intimacy with . . . who knew? At least one girl, maybe several. Maybe many. I didn't know anything about him anymore.

"Mom, say something." Pale and shaken, Justin gripped the doorjamb beside him.

Terrible thoughts came to me. Was he a bad seed, like his father? I was sure I was a bad mother. Would he ever amount to anything?

My chest pounded, my breath accelerated. Oh, God, I was having a heart attack. How could this be happening? My beautiful baby. He wouldn't go to college now. He probably didn't even care.

Pull it together, Nicole. What had Justin done, really? He hadn't broken any laws. He hadn't hurt anyone. But he'd had sex and might now pay the terrible price of becoming a father at sixteen.

Daniela began to babble. "I'm so sorry. It just happened. I don't blame my parents for hating me. I hate myself."

I looked at this girl I'd known for four hours, saw her wide, terrified eyes, and all I could think was, *They told her parents first.* Anger began to boil just below my hurt and panic.

"I need to speak to Justin alone."

Daniela tearfully left us. Justin sat down on the bed next to me, and after a minute, I put my arms around him and he put his head on my shoulder. And he cried. I cried too. Midge and Margo plowed their heads into our laps, and we all sat pressed against each other, my heart taking comfort from the thought that at least I felt close to him again, and we would solve this problem together.

"How far along is she?" I asked, my thoughts toward Daniela turning dark. *That little . . .* She had done this to my son. Lured him into her snare and ruined his life.

"Not far. She got a pregnancy test right away, because, well, she was worried. Then, her mom saw the pregnancy kit in the trash."

They hadn't told her parents first, or even at all! I was the one they'd come to for help. I allowed myself a small burst of optimism. We would handle this. We would come out stronger for it.

"We'll go to Planned Parenthood," I said. "There's plenty of time. I'll help you take her and pay for it—"

"No."

I stopped short. "What do you mean, no?"

Justin squirmed away from me, moving so we could face each

other, and raised a hand to rub his eye, which had begun to twitch. "I mean, Daniela doesn't want to . . . you know . . . end it."

Oh, she didn't, did she? There were a lot of things I didn't want, either, and one was to see my son's future go down the drain. Or mine, for that matter.

Then my stomach rolled, sickening me. What was I thinking? This was my grandchild; I didn't want to see this pregnancy ended.

Although, that might be better for Justin.

Grating my teeth, I tried to speak pleasantly. "Are you saying she wants to put it up for adoption?" I knew immediately I could never live with that, either. If they dared to give away my grandchild, I thought wildly, I would adopt the baby myself.

"She wants to keep it, Mom. She wants to raise it." A whole range of expressions moved across Justin's face—anger, fear, resignation.

"Justin, is it possible that you're not the father, that it's really some other boy?" I stood up then and began pacing the small room.

Justin shook his head, exasperated. "I don't know who it would be. The only guys she hangs with at school, besides me, are my friends, and they're not . . ." He broke off. "Anyway, lying isn't Daniela's style."

"But you used contraception, right?"

"A condom."

"What about her?"

His eyes grew round. "Isn't the condom enough?"

"Not always!" I knew that for sure. The mere fact that Justin was here, living and breathing, proved that condoms sometimes failed. And a failure like that, I also knew for sure, could strike the death blow to a dying marriage.

And yet, I could never think of my son's existence as any kind of failure. He was the best thing in my life.

"Do you love this girl?"

He sighed heavily. "I was into her. She was fun. But I didn't think . . . I didn't expect . . ."

I shook my head. Of course he hadn't.

Justin had retreated to a blank stare that made me think of the joke my sister and I used to make as kids when something was unfathomably strange or incomprehensible. Using our best robot arms and voices, we would say, "This. Does. Not. Compute. This. Does. Not. Compute."

Other thoughts blew through my mind. Justin's child. My grandchild. Ten or fifteen years from now, it would have been the world's most precious gift, a blessing. But here, now, at our ages, it was a catastrophe.

I'd been a mother at twenty-two. The explosions and aftershocks from my failed relationships had persisted into my late twenties. Career? I didn't even start to earn a proper living until my thirties.

And what about my poor son, who was only sixteen? If I couldn't wrap my mind around this disaster, how could Justin?

"Who does Daniela think is going to help her if she keeps the baby?" I asked. "Who's going to stay up nights? And pay for everything?"

I was. I could just see it. The truth was, I would do it in a heartbeat. But I would also grieve for my lost plans and dreams. Frustration and rage were building. "She has no idea what she's in for."

Justin shot up from the bed, startling Midge and Margo, who jumped to their feet and slunk from the room. "What do you want me to do, Mom?" he cried out. "I'm, like, a pawn here. I feel responsible for this, but I don't get to decide anything!"

Sudden exhaustion swept over me. I wanted to put my head down and go to sleep. But I needed answers first. "How did you and Daniela get together?"

He sighed, as if he needed to gather his strength. "Remember that night in October when I came home at two in the morning and you were pissed off?"

I gave him a dour look. "You told me you were at that rich boy's party. Vincent's. Are you telling me now you were with Daniela?"

"I *was* at Vincent's house! Somebody gave roofies to a couple of girls from Hollywood High, and all these stories were going around. Daniela was there, and we were talking. She was new at Laurelmont, and she didn't know that many people. I warned her about the roofies. I said she should get out of there, and I ended up driving her home."

A drop of sweat trickled down my back. "And you had sex with her?" Had he been fornicating and lying to my face for seven months?

"Mom, no!" Justin turned to face me, gazing earnestly into my eyes. "That night, we just talked for a long time in my car. But I kept seeing her around, and we would talk. We got along."

"Apparently so."

His lips tightening, he gave me a resentful sideways glance.

I could feel my blood pounding in my ears. "Are you *kidding*? You're looking *offended* at me? After what's happened?"

"Look," he said. "Kids hook up all the time. And, yeah, we hooked up. But we like each other too."

"Hooked up. What does that even mean?"

He sighed deeply and rolled his eyes, as if he was deciding to humor me. "Hooking up, Mom. You know, making out, fooling around, whatever."

I thought of all the dark, little-used trails of Laurel Canyon, perfect for nefarious deeds and teen canoodling. Caroline and I had used a few of them ourselves in high school. Why did that seem so much more innocent? "And . . . you? Did this?"

"It's no big deal, Mom." Justin gave me his look of supreme boredom.

This was my honors student, the boy who hand-made me cards for Mother's Day. He was the boy all the moms loved—so polite, they said, and such a good example for their sons.

I wanted to tear my hair and clothes and throw myself on a bonfire.

Justin stood and headed for the door. On his way out, he turned to me, showing me the face of a person I'd never seen. "You wanna talk to Daniela now?"

Chapter 6

We found her asleep on the sofa. Without a glance in my direction, he laid a blanket gently across her shoulders and went to his bedroom. During the night, it stormed and thundered, proof that the gods were angry with the wicked children under my care. And probably with me as well.

I'd been so blind.

The next morning, the sofa was empty, the sheets and blanket neatly folded. Daniela was nowhere to be found, and Justin's bedroom door was closed.

I went into a slow burn. I'd bet she was in there with him. In *his* bed, under *my* roof, after all the trouble they'd caused. And after Justin *promised!* I could have simply opened the door and checked, but my own mixed feelings on the subject stopped me.

Speaking as a mother, I didn't think kids should lie to their parents. In fairness, however, I had to admit that Caroline and I had done it. As teenagers, we were still reeling from the death of our mom, the maker and enforcer of rules, the glue that had held our household together.

Although it didn't seem that way to me at the time, we pushed some things to the limit, lying to my widowed father like two undercover operatives. Convinced that she had met her soul mate, Caroline was sleeping with her True Love Grant at fifteen, while I skipped school occasionally, dating guys and going to parties that Dad didn't know about.

And yet, we were good girls too. We maintained a B average, stayed out of trouble, didn't drink or do drugs—at least, not to excess. It was just that parents got so picky and annoying about little things that were no big deal, like a party with no parental supervision or groups of teens riding around in cars. It was easier to just do what you wanted and bend the truth than to deal with a parent's hang-ups.

Now, I understood why parents were the way they were, because they knew what could happen and they worried. But at the time, my dad had just seemed neurotic to me. As I probably seemed to Justin. Which is why I told him not to lie and forgave him when he did.

And why I felt entitled to *know* when he did.

So I resorted to the trick I'd used back when I thought Justin was smoking weed with his friends: spying from the bushes outside his bedroom window.

In case I got caught, I would arm myself with a scissor and claim to be cutting flowers for the table.

I tromped across the wet grass and around the side of the house. The rosebushes had grown dense and were packed with thorns, not to mention soaked. Justin's shade was half up, meaning I'd be able to see in if I could just get close enough.

I sucked in my breath and tried to wiggle through a tiny space between two bushes, immediately drenching my shirt. The thorns caught at the fabric and tore it. Darn it! Just as I got close to the house, I saw Daniela in the yard. Her back to me, she sat on a yoga pad on the grass in a meditation pose, cross-legged, her hands on her knees, palms up. She sat immobile, straight-backed, graceful. Mike's dogs ambled around her, sniffing the ground.

Daniela was close enough to hear my rustlings from the bushes. I hurriedly snipped some roses to authenticate my alibi, then tried to get out. Thorns had snagged me from several directions, holding me in one place. Darn it again!

"What did Justin do this time?"

I jumped, tearing my blouse on another thorn. "Caroline!"

Judging from her downcast eyes and the dejected slope of

her mouth, I guessed she was still in a state of extreme suffering. Despite her troubles, she gamely waded into the bushes and helped extricate me.

Although she was a year older than I was, people sometimes thought we were twins. We had the same wavy auburn hair, the hazel eyes that turned green in sunlight, and our mother's hourglass figure, with its small waist, full chest, and round bottom. Caroline hated the look, wanting to be rail thin for the fashionable fitted shapes and short hemlines that she loved. I, on the other hand, always kind of liked being curvy. It went with my hippie-style, soft, flowy dresses.

As we emerged from the rosebushes, Daniela stirred from her trance, stretching her arms up to the sky and coming to her feet. She walked over to us.

"Caroline, this is Daniela, Justin's . . . friend," I announced as I checked my watch. "You and Justin leave for school in thirty minutes." Judging by the look Caroline gave me, I must have barked the words out like a drill sergeant.

"I'll go wake him up," Daniela was quick to offer.

"Nope! I'll be doing that."

I charged into the house followed by my wide-eyed sister. "What's going on?" she asked.

I pounded on Justin's door, then took off for the kitchen. "I have bad news," I warned.

"So do I."

"I'll win this one." I pulled out two of my signature latte bowls and two spoons and clattered them all onto the counter.

She grimaced, giving me her answer in a singsong voice. "I don't *think so.*"

We had to wait until the kids had taken off in Justin's rattletrap car, eating the peanut butter bagels I'd made for them. Finally, I filled our bowls with espresso and steamed milk, and we settled at the picnic table under the trees. Only in the worst of weather did this household eat indoors.

"So who goes first?" Caroline asked. The one with the worst news always went first.

We stared at each other.

"Let's go together," I said as two hummingbirds circled overhead, dipping their beaks into the jasmine blossoms. "On the count of three. One, two, three . . . Justin got a girl pregnant."

"I have to sell my share of the house."

The two horrible pieces of information hung in the air until Caroline said, "You win."

Her news was pretty bad, though. We had grown up in this house, sleeping in bunk beds in the space that Justin's twin bed now occupied, while our parents had the bedroom that was now mine. Maybe that's why we'd practically lived outdoors, eating at the picnic table, napping in the hammock beneath the big oak tree, because the house was small for four people. Then my mother died when I was ten and Caroline was almost twelve. Our dad died when Justin was three.

Caroline and I had co-owned the house ever since. We'd agreed that I would live there rent-free but pay both her and my share of the property taxes. So I got a lovely, low-cost place to live, while she got a valuable investment with no out-of-pocket expenses.

"You can't sell half a house!" I exclaimed in response. "And besides, I don't want to own this place with some stranger."

There was clearly no question of my buying her out.

Last month, Grant had simply packed a couple of bags and left town, saying he had "things to think about."

"I'm broke," Caroline said. "There's no income since the business died. Grant's back in town and has this idea we can stay together in our house." She and Grant owned a little bungalow in Beachwood Canyon. "But I just can't . . . if we're not . . ." She dissolved into tears. "I have to find a place of my own and I've never lived by myself."

"Stay here. With us. I'd love it, actually." I spoke unhesitatingly, from my heart. This was my sister, for Pete's sake.

"You barely have enough room as it is." She looked tempted, though.

"What do you mean? Justin and I each have our own room. We'll put you on the screened porch and hang up drapes or something for privacy." It was settled as far as I was concerned.

"Oh, Nicki, I'm so sad." Caroline wept bitter tears while I patted her on the back, not sure what to do for her. Then she gave her head an impatient little shake.

"Anyway, my God, here I am just talking about myself. Tell me about Justin. Was that girl the baby mama? She's pregnant?"

"So I'm told." It still didn't seem real to me.

"And our little Justin is having sex?" Caroline's face reflected both amusement and dismay.

I returned a sour face of my own. "Hooking up," I corrected her.

"Is that different from having sex?"

"I think having sex is a subset of hooking up."

"The things you learn." Caroline did not have children. She sat back. "But, Nicki, a little grandson or granddaughter! You're only thirty-eight. Think of it. It could be almost like a second child for you." Her voice was wistful.

"No, you think of it! Justin saddled with a baby at sixteen. By the time his friends settle down with babies, he'll have a teenager. How will he apply to colleges next year and graduate from high school? How will he *go* to college?"

"With the help of his family. And Daniela's." She gave me a hopeful, encouraging smile.

"Daniela's family." I told my sister what they'd done while she listened in horror. "They'll come around, though," I said.

"You think?"

"They can't completely abandon their young pregnant daughter, can they? I mean, who does that?"

Chapter 7

I remember the day in my freshman year of high school, Caroline's sophomore year, when she told me she'd met an "older man."

"His name's Grant," she said. He was seventeen and already a senior.

"He must be really smart," I said, thrilled for my sister.

"He's *super* smart." He was cute too, she informed me, filling me in on his plaid shirts and the way his hair feathered around his neck. "And he has his driver's license!"

"That's so cool!" I could see why she liked him.

And he continued to impress, as he arrived that weekend to take Caroline to the Arclight in Hollywood to see *Forrest Gump.* Since this was the olden days, before every last person had a navigational system, my dad had speculated hopefully that Grant would not be able to locate our tiny unmarked road and find his way through the potholes and underbrush to our house. He was having doubts about his fifteen-year-old daughter dating a boy who was six months away from going to college.

Little did my father know that Caroline had prepped Grant with meticulous directions. "Go exactly two miles on Laurel Canyon Boulevard. When you see a brick fence, slow down, because you're close. Turn at a little road that's on your left only. There's no name placard, but you'll see a rusty mailbox hanging from its post; turn and follow the road on up, even when it looks like a cow path and you think you must be lost. Just keep going up, up, up until you reach a flat area where you can park."

Grant stepped out of the car looking crisp, relaxed, and very debonair to my fourteen-year-old eyes.

"You made it." My dad looked half-impressed, half-disappointed. "Right on time."

"Yes, sir!" Grant made it sound like, *Of course. Was there ever any doubt?*

Right from the beginning, Grant and Caroline were a team, working smoothly together, making it easier for one another to go through life.

They were my standard for compatibility—seamless perfection. They agreed on most things, went everywhere together, loved and trusted each other completely, and never appeared to suffer the agonies of doubt and insecurity that the rest of us faced. Anything less than that, I always thought, meant you were *all wrong* for each other.

In high school, I knew the boys I dated were all wrong for me. Trevor, who talked endlessly about himself; Wade, whose world started and ended with the swim team; Brennan, who I was pretty sure really liked boys but hadn't admitted it to himself yet.

Practice guys, Jamie called them. They were a waste of time, siphoning my energy away from productive activities I enjoyed, like painting watercolors, designing T-shirts, and working on the school yearbook.

In my freshman year of college, it was more of the same: quiet, boring Henry, followed by Ben, the union buster, who really wanted an activist girlfriend, then by Ahmed, the visitor to this country who really wanted a green card.

I was done with practicing. I was ready for the real thing, but how to find it? It wasn't like having food delivered. I couldn't just order up a guy according to specifications.

So I back-burnered the notion of dating, hung out with my girlfriends, immersed myself in schoolwork, and began to volunteer for a local animal shelter.

And as things worked out, this was when Mike came into my life.

Chapter 8

Caroline protested for only a moment before accepting my invitation to move in. She headed for the screened porch with a bucket and a mop, while I went to the small separate building that I'd had built for my ceramics studio.

I stood there looking at the place where I had spent so many hours. At the potter's wheel and chair with tables on either side. At the labeled shelves with pieces at all phases of construction: those waiting to be bisque-fired, then glazed, then fired again; finished pieces; and those unfortunates under the sign Adopt Me. Those were the ones with defects so small you would never notice them, but large enough that I couldn't in good conscience sell them.

It was all so familiar to me and was a real source of pride. No one else I knew from my art and ceramics classes had been able to figure out how to make a living from the things we created. I hadn't had to sell myself to the devil, either; luckily, there were people out there willing to buy the pieces I chose to make, exactly as I chose to make them.

Yet, I'd kept my own name out of it, selling all my plates, bowls, vases, and candlesticks under the name Clayworks.

And now it was time to put the name Nicole Adams out there. I had six weeks to make my own personal statement about how we live. What on earth would I do?

First of all, what did I think about how we lived? About how I lived? Two days ago, my ideas about life had been easily described: simple. Today, I no longer knew anything.

A strange combination of apprehension and delight crept over me as I thought of Justin and Daniela's announcement. A grandchild! I could almost hear baby squeals and laughter, feel the softness of baby cheeks. This child would take over my life, but in what way I didn't know. It would be a joy but would also likely drain my energy and creativity, not to mention my savings. It might kill any chance I had of becoming an artist. No sooner had I had that thought than my mind flew to Justin. This was so much worse for him. His youth, his chances for college and a career, all inevitably altered forever. The anger I'd been feeling gave way to grief. And fear.

Who was I kidding? I had ten Clayworks orders to produce before my next ship date. I had a credit card payment to make, extra mouths to feed. Panic rose over me like a wave in a storm.

Within moments, I was at my potter's wheel filling an order for a table service for eight, the tension in my shoulders subsiding, the stiffness in my neck slipping away. No matter how bad things were, I was at peace at the wheel. There I could dissolve into pure sensory experience: the steady whirring sound, the movement of the clay and its smooth coolness. I focused on how it felt, the exact diameter of the plate, the angle at which the lip curled up on the edges. It was almost impossible to produce identical pieces of ceramics by hand, and yet I could come close if I followed the memory of it in my hands and fingers.

It took utter, complete focus on a single thing.

I had never understood the concept of multitasking. I put the parts of my life into boxes and handled one at a time. Pick up one box, attend to the matters inside, finish what you can, put the box away. Then move on to the next. And always make sure that each and every box was light enough and small enough to handle alone.

I had some boxes dedicated to my marriage to Brady, boxes that I'd wound round and round with packing tape, sealing every opening, and hidden in a back corner of my mind that I rarely visited. I had other mental boxes in my life, like for my finances and for my friends and family. There was a number of Justin boxes, for things like day-to-day well-being, or his academic life and college admissions. These were always open and out on a nearby shelf in my brain.

As for Mike, some of his boxes stayed well-sealed, while on others, the tape had lost its glue from being pulled off and put back on so many times. All the Mike boxes were off to the side, hidden from view but easy enough to reach if I wanted. Even if I never did, I could.

And finally, I had a single box for my dream of becoming an artist, containing a jumble of ideas and objects that I'd used for inspiration.

Enough of dreams and inspiration. I didn't have time for art right now. I needed money.

And so, I remained in my mental box for my Clayworks ceramics. I stopped thinking about my exciting new opportunity at the museum and the homeless girl who had entered my life with her illegitimate spawn—my grandchild. Working at a steady pace, I reentered my serene place, producing eight virtually identical dinner plates, one after the other, and then eight virtually identical salad plates. Pleased with myself, I set them aside. I would use my special-formula glaze that I called Not Your Ordinary Eggshell White, because of its particular depth and iridescence, which set it apart from the other products out there. My custom-formulated glazes, which I'd patented upon my father's advice, were one of the reasons for the success of my business.

Finished for the day, I wandered out to see how Caroline was settling into the house she had left so many years ago to marry her soul mate. The house to which she was now returning. I wouldn't say it to her, but I'd say it to myself, with regret.

Love doesn't last.

I told you so.

After high school, Grant had gone to MIT, mainly due to pressure from his folks, but within a year had transferred to Cal Tech, unwilling to be separated from Caroline while she was finishing high school. Three years later, at the ages of twenty-two and nineteen, Grant and Caroline announced—to a general outcry of protest—that they were getting married. My dad and the Harpers, Grant's parents, all thought they were too young. My dad just wanted them to be sure not to rush things. Mr. and Mrs. Harper had darker motives, I thought, dropping hints that Caroline was dragging down their brilliant son, the ascending star. He'd already been developing apps for years and was talking about starting a high-tech business with friends.

If Mom had still been alive, she would have kept everyone on their best behavior. Instead, Grant almost came to blows with his father over the wedding date. Caroline didn't speak to our own father for a month, while, in his own ineffectual way, he tried to enlist me into talking her out of the whole thing.

Poor Dad. On this issue, he was, by his standards, putting up a good fight. However, I knew a losing battle when I saw one.

"You may be right, Dad," I told him. "Maybe she is too young, but she's going to do this, no matter how we feel. We have two choices: we go along with it, or they get married without us."

Grant and Caroline were married in our backyard, with the parents in attendance. The day was sunny, and smog clogged our little slice-shaped view of the city. Undeterred, we took our wedding photos against the bougainvillea that hung low over the trellised patio, creating a festive backdrop of greenery and purple blossoms.

The beaming groom wore a gray suit, the blooming bride a white eyelet dress that floated around her and white rosebuds in her hair. I served as maid of honor, best man, and ring bearer, wearing a pale-yellow dress. The guests were limited to family, close friends, and our dogs at the time, Ruthy and Waldo, both golden retrievers.

We played Bruce Springsteen, ate egg rolls, and drank champagne, while I snapped photos of the jubilant bride and groom, so absolutely certain that nothing could ever dim their love for one another. I wondered how they could be so sure and crossed my fingers for them. But mainly, I was happy for my sister.

"You look so beautiful today," I told her.

She threw her arms around me. "You're next!"

"I don't want to be next. I'm not ready."

"You just haven't met the right guy."

"That's for sure." I wouldn't dream of reciting vows of love and loyalty to any of my practice guys.

Caroline just looked at me. "I promise you. When you meet him, you'll know."

Having completed the dinnerware set, I was calm as I walked from my studio across the yard and into the house to join my sister. Yesterday, when I'd received that enormous new box labeled DANIELA, it had loomed dangerously large and menacing, far too worrisome to face. For now, I would keep it on a back shelf in my mental closet, but high enough to see it in case I needed to find it.

It was five o'clock, much later than I'd realized. "Nicki, come see what I'm doing!" Caroline called out. She had scrubbed the floors of the porch and dusted and was now inspecting the inside of a small wardrobe. "It doesn't quite meet my need for hanging space, but I can fold the rest of my things into some flat under-the-bed organizers, and"—she snapped her fingers—"problem solved!" Two spots of color had risen on her cheeks as she surveyed her progress.

"That's wonderful!" I looked around to see how I could make her more comfortable. The screen windows would only work for the summer months; I would have to get glass windows put in this fall. Yikes, another expense. I felt my chest flutter.

No matter, I told myself. If my sister was okay, I was okay. I knew that by tomorrow she'd be into my bureau, sorting my socks by length and color, but it was fine. It made her happy.

"Mom?" Justin's furious voice floated over my left shoulder. He must have been arriving home late from school. "What's going on here?"

"Sweetheart!" I turned to give him a hug, just barely registering the fact that Daniela was here again, standing behind him. "I have great news. Your Auntie Caroline's coming to live with us!"

Justin's narrow face was tight with fatigue and stress. "When did you decide this?"

"Just this morning."

"What about Daniela?"

I didn't answer. Daniela had a family of her own. She wasn't my responsibility.

A second later, everyone was talking. Daniela was saying, "I can stay with Heather," while Justin growled, "You're staying with us," and Caroline was saying, "I think I should go," while I snapped, "No, you're my sister!" The dogs started barking, ending any hope of us hearing each other.

Justin scowled at me. Everything was so screwed up.

I fixed a hard stare upon my son.

Chapter 9

"Let's take a walk," I said to him. Neither of us speaking, we trudged through the yard and out the side gate to the Trail of Terror. Due to the steep canyon hillsides everywhere, it was the only place available for us to walk.

Justin and I had done this many times. Appreciating the last bits of daylight on this evening in early May, we set off down the road, the dogs trailing behind us. Since the traffic was nonexistent, we didn't bother with leashes.

Our little road started and branched off from Laurel Canyon Boulevard, which was the major artery of the canyon, snaking its way from Hollywood Boulevard north over the hill and into the San Fernando Valley. As you came up the Trail of Terror, the first house you saw (or rather, the first mailbox, because you couldn't actually see the house) belonged to a famous German director of horror films, who lived there along with his aging basset hound, Wolfgang. His name was Stefan Richter.

Neighbors for the last twenty years, he and I had tried to engage in a friendly annual competition as to who could throw the most parties each year. Until, that is, we realized that our partying styles were totally different. He was the clear winner for big events—bashes featuring open bars, valet parking, groups of celebrities and the paparazzi that came with them. I, however, crushed Stefan for small dinner parties, potluck gatherings, impromptu evenings where whoever was around stayed to dinner. He made sure to invite me to his things and knew a place at my table was always set for him.

He and I also took care of each other. I looked after Wolfgang when Stefan was away and watered his plants when his housekeeper was gone. He sent his workers over to help me clean drain gutters and fix broken stuff around the house.

Stefan had originally owned a small house like mine, but later, as his career flourished, he had bought an adjacent lot and built what could only be called a compound—a main house of four thousand square feet, two guesthouses, a pool and tennis court, and more.

His place was modest by Hollywood standards but palatial compared to ours, which was the only house after his along the Trail of Terror. Stefan had also started to maintain the first quarter mile of road up to his house with two nicely paved lanes, street lighting, and neatly trimmed foliage. The remaining three-quarters of a mile of road were my responsibility and virtually unchanged since the days of my childhood, hence the definite sense as you drove uphill that you were headed for the wrong side of town. The two lanes narrowed to a single poorly paved track, the streetlights disappeared, and the bushes loomed into the path, making it even narrower.

Justin launched in. "You didn't even think of how I felt! You didn't talk to me before you asked Auntie to live with us."

Rats. Here I'd been preparing to climb up onto my high horse and call him on his mistakes, but he'd beaten me to it. He was right too. I should have asked him.

"Okay, I'm sorry, but she's sleeping on her friend's floor right now. I can't say no to her." The dogs bounded ahead of us, even though we walked in big strides, practically running downhill. I should have been finding this part of it easy, but Justin set a fast pace.

"We have to help Daniela," he insisted.

Boy, was I out of shape. My breathing was already speeding up. "Honey, Daniela's a minor with some very big decisions to make right now. She needs her family."

"They aren't there for her." Seeing me huff and puff, Justin slowed and leaned down to pick up a stone in the road. He cradled it in his hand.

"Not now, but we'll hope they come to their senses and take her back." Gratefully, I stopped walking and bent over, my hands on my knees.

Justin threw the stone into the canyon. "So let's help her out, at least until her folks stop acting like dicks."

I sighed. "I hate to get involved. Those people don't seem very reasonable."

"We're already involved." Justin's voice filled with regret. He stared up at the sky, which was starting to darken. "I'm sorry, Mom. I'm really sorry for all this."

I patted his arm. "It'll be okay." I didn't exactly know how it would be okay, but I'd always done that for Justin, especially when he was little, making sure I stayed calm, upbeat, and cheerful so he would feel safe. "I promise, it'll be okay."

"You always say that, Mom." Justin grinned down at me, and it warmed my heart to finally see him smile. "A tsunami could be coming at us full force, and you'd be saying, 'We're okay!'"

"If a tsunami were coming at us full force, I'd be telling you to dog paddle. I'm not stupid." I laughed along with him, feeling better. I could keep it together through anything so long as Justin and I were fine.

"But why can't Daniela stay here for now?" Justin persisted.

"Maybe she can. But I'd prefer you not having sex with her in our house."

"I know." Justin picked up a stick and called for the dogs. "Mom, I get it. I messed up. I'm trying to do the right thing. Don't you think I owe it to Daniela to help her?"

He threw the stick toward Midge and Margo, who had reappeared down where the road curved. They raced toward it, scuffling over it in the growing darkness.

He was standing by this girl in the only way he knew how: to offer her his home. I nodded slowly. "Yes, I see what you're saying."

The dogs exploded into barking and took off again, disappearing around the curve.

"Darn," I said. "We need to go back." I flipped on a flashlight I always took with me on the Trail of Terror and shone it down the road. Empty, it vanished around a bend.

Justin called to them. "Midge! Margo!" We waited, but the barking only intensified.

"There must be a car on the road," Justin said.

I didn't like that. A few years ago, a pullout area had become a place of business for some of Hollywood's drug dealers. They were gone now, but I kept an eye out for strangers. I pulled a dog whistle from my pocket and blasted it.

The dogs, out of sight, continued to bark. It was almost completely dark now.

"Honestly!" I trudged down the hill toward the dogs and rounded the turn, Justin on my heels. We arrived in time to see a blue car disappear down the hill in the beam of the flashlight, the dogs behind it, their barking now frantic and high-pitched. My light played on the trees and the empty, pitted road, which once again curved out of sight in front of us.

"Huh." Justin stared down the road as far as he could. "It must have been coming up and then turned around. I wonder what it was doing all the way up here?" Because ours was the only house on this last length of road, this meant that any car driving up here was hopelessly lost, coming to see us, or deliberately cruising for trouble.

"Well, it's gone now." I blew the dog whistle again. The darkness pressing in around us, I could see only Justin and the empty road in our single tunnel of light.

A few seconds later, the dogs appeared.

"Come! We're going home!" I yelled, and the four of us started back up the road together.

"So how about Daniela takes the porch and Caroline and I

share my bedroom?" I suggested. "Temporarily." My heart sank a little at the thought, but I told myself I could handle any inconvenience for a short time.

"No way," Justin shot back, sounding almost cheerful. "I've got it all worked out. Auntie takes the porch, Daniela takes my room, and I take the living room sofa."

"That's very sweet, but you don't have to punish yourself."

"It's not a punishment. It's just the way it needs to be." Justin's tone left no room for argument.

I didn't think he would get a good night's sleep on the sofa, but there wasn't much I could do about it right now. And besides, I told myself, it was temporary.

Chapter 10

That night, I opened Mike's gift, a little package neatly wrapped in brown paper and tied with a piece of raffia.

It was a silver chain, its links forged into a simple braid. My breath caught. I slid it over my head, then looked in the mirror.

It was perfect, a small thing that Mike had known I would like. He picked these things up for me as thank-yous or birthday offerings. I had told him it wasn't necessary, but he persisted. "I would buy you flowers, but you grow your own," he explained.

I pecked out a text. *So pretty—you always know.* Then, after a moment's hesitation, I deleted the second sentence and wrote, *Thank you.*

It had all started soon after Caroline's wedding when I was a sophomore at Cal State Northridge. Jamie, my roommate at the time, had gotten as a birthday present a free intro lesson for two at Climb, one of the early rock climbing gyms in Los Angeles. Assigned as freshman dorm roommates, Jamie and I had ended up getting an apartment together for our sophomore and junior years as well. Jamie was fun, spontaneous, and up for anything. She was pumped about this rock climbing thing. She made me come along, protesting.

"You may climb alone," I warned Jamie. Clinging onto minuscule plastic handholds while fifty feet in the air was not what I usually aspired to.

We stood below a series of enormous pale-gray walls pocked with hand and foot holds of every color, some of the walls folded like a giant accordion, some gently rippling, some almost vertical. The wall directly before us sloped backward, which decreased its steepness. Markers bearing numbers indicated that the climbs on this wall were relatively easy, although they looked terrifying to me.

Spotting a name tag on a red-shirted employee, Jamie said, "That's our instructor! Zane!" She waved to get his attention.

Zane, predictably, was sun-browned, well-muscled, and friendly. Straps and metal loops, the things that kept him from death, swung from a harness around his waist and thighs.

I had noticed, on many walls, the climbers used harnesses and ropes and were helped by people on the ground who held the ropes and eased the climbers down slowly if they fell.

That made sense to me. If I had to enter places where humans were never intended to go, I could do with a few precautions.

Zane showed us some basic footholds and how to traverse, which meant how to crab along sideways, essentially practicing your climbing while remaining two feet off the ground.

This I could do. I went back and forth a few times, bravely putting my fingernails, if not the rest of me, at risk, then began to pine for a long, tall, cool one at the Toehold Bar near the entrance. But Zane and Jamie had just begun. "Come on!" Jamie yelled, waving to me to climb higher.

"What about our ropes?" I asked Zane, only to be informed, "You don't need ropes for this wall. Follow me!" Like a squirrel in a tree, he scampered upward.

It seemed like a poor idea, but I tried. Tentatively, I latched onto a handhold, hauled myself up, then caught a toehold and climbed higher. Another handhold . . . this wasn't so bad! "Hey, look at me!" I yelled up to Jamie.

"Awesome," she yelled back.

I crawled higher. The handholds were smaller now, the toeholds farther apart. I had to be twenty feet in the air. No, probably a hundred. *Good enough*, I decided. I'd gone so much higher than I'd expected. I would call it a day. My right foot reached for a toehold, but those directly below me seemed to have melted away. Where was that green one?

I looked down.

Whoa. My stomach somersaulted as the whole hillside slanted alarmingly, becoming impossibly steep. The candy-colored protrusions for my hands and feet, which had seemed adequate before, had shrunk to the size of M&M's.

"Jamie! Help!" I gasped out, clinging to the tiny nubs of plastic.

"You go, girl!" she yelled merrily from her spot at least eight hundred feet above me.

A bead of sweat rolled down my forehead and off the tip of my nose, plunging into the abyss below. My right foot flailed uselessly, seeking a safe toehold below me. I tried to move my hands down, but they refused to detach themselves from their current safety zones.

"Behind you!" Three guys pulled level with me. The two farthest away passed me, climbing steadily, while the one closest to me glanced over, then came to an abrupt halt. "You okay?"

"Well . . ." I squeaked, "I'd be better if I were on the ground." My hand slipped off one of the plastic handholds, and I moaned. "I can't look down!"

In my dizziness and fear, my vision had narrowed into a tunnel directly in front of me. Unable to see where to put my hands and feet, I remained where I was, paralyzed, sure I was riveted to this spot for the rest of time.

The stranger moved in behind me, close enough for me to feel his lips next to my ear as he spoke. "You'll be fine. Just grab on here." He moved my right hand to a gray protuberance, which I clung to.

"Now your left foot goes here." He pointed to an orange nub that, in my feverish peripheral vision, seemed about ten feet away.

"You're joking."

"May I?" He closed his hand around my ankle and guided

my foot down. "Now your left hand." His fingers on my wrist, he somehow got that moved as well.

Little by little, he guided me down, staying close behind me. I couldn't see him but heard and felt him acutely, his voice that of a young man, his breath pepperminty, his hands strong and confident.

When we reached the bottom, I leaned back against his chest for a moment, feeling my head rest on his shoulder. His hands came around my waist.

I turned around.

Steel-blue eyes and a gap between his two front teeth. His mouth curled up in one corner.

"Can I buy you a drink? I owe you at least that much for saving my life." This I said while thinking, *Who are you, anyway? Don't go.* He was cute, but more than that, he had a self-assurance that caught my attention. He was a guy who knew who he was and where he was going.

He hesitated, glancing up toward his two friends waving from the top of the wall. "We were warming up for a climb." Apparently, this wall that had so terrified me was what this guy used to work the kinks out before a real climb. "But . . ." His eyes swept over me. "I suppose I could catch up with them later."

By the time we left, he had gotten my phone number. Two days later, he called to ask me out. And that was how I met Mike, beginning the most important friendship of my life.

Chapter 11

Daniela was a funny kid with quirky interests that she'd taught herself from Youtube, like knitting and ballroom dancing. She had spent two nights under my roof, helping with the dogs and the dishes, good-naturedly letting Caroline organize her closet and volunteering for unpopular chores like cleaning the toilets. We all liked her for her easygoing sweetness and willingness to pitch in.

No surprise that my anger about our situation found its focus not on her, but on her parents. I could not forget the pain in her eyes and voice that first night. *They threw me out.* I believed it was a privilege to have kids. Kids were about hope and the future. They were too young to be blamed for anything. It was we adults who had screwed up this world, and the least we could do as parents was to refrain from making things worse by screwing our kids up too.

It was eight o'clock on a Saturday morning, and instead of peacefully reflecting over my morning latte, I was shaking with outrage. On Daniela's behalf and also on mine.

I needed to speak with them, anyway; I would go and pay them a visit. It was an unconventional time to drop in, I knew, but they'd already failed to return a series of phone calls. At this time, they would likely be home.

Harris. That was the name. I reached for the school directory, which would have their home address.

An hour later, I pulled up at their home, then rechecked the house number. Yes, this was it.

I stared at the house. The word ugly applied, and yet seemed inadequate to the task of describing this house, puny in the face of the pure dread that it inspired in me. Not just dread, but fear, claustrophobia, and an intense need to be somewhere else.

The walls were a bubblegum-pink stucco, the heavily textured kind that would cause abrasions if you brushed against it. A bunker-like building, essentially a giant shoebox, it had only a few small windows and a small door, trimmed in white. Even worse was the yard, which consisted of white-painted gravel that covered every available surface, from the base of the house to the curb, uninterrupted by anything green. The gravel, along with the darkened windows and a few dead bushes that clung to the house's perimeter, all gave the impression that nothing living existed within twenty-five feet of this place, inside or out.

Nothing living, and yet the house itself almost shimmered with a strange life force. The giant pink shoebox seemed to hunker down, malevolent, squinting at me with its little window eyes, checking me out.

The hair on my arms rose. What had I thought to accomplish in coming here alone? I should have waited for Mike to come home. A black belt in kung fu, aikido, and tae kwon do, he'd be handy to have beside me right now.

I wanted to be in a normal place, where I felt safe, surrounded by people I loved and trusted.

There were no cars parked curbside in front of the house or in the driveway. Where could these people be so early on a Saturday? Did I care? No. In fact, relief flooded me.

No one was home. I would have to leave. Immediately.

I pulled my car forward and completed a U-turn just in time to see a black sedan weaving in my direction. I pulled over as far to the right as I could and parked across the street, as if I were visiting neighbors and not the Harrises. I pulled out my phone and busily pretended to text someone.

The black car hit the curb, went over it, then pulled crookedly into the Harrises' driveway, coming to a rest at an awkward twenty-five degrees off normal. Hands trembling, I slid lower in my seat, feigning total absorption in my phone.

The driver's door opened and a man half fell into the driveway. Although his face was turned away, I caught a glimpse of dark-blond curls. He regained his footing, then fell again, sprawling into the gravel and swearing as he scraped his hands and knees. After a moment, he stood and, holding onto the car for stability, proceeded along its side.

With careful, wobbly steps, the man was trying to traverse the empty space between his car and the front door. He eventually made it and spent some time fishing for his key and fitting it into the door lock. He disappeared inside.

My jaw clenched as I tried to think of some reason why this man, totally polluted at nine in the morning, wasn't who I thought he was, why he wasn't Daniela's father.

I couldn't. He had a key to her house. But still . . . *innocent until proven guilty*, I told myself.

I started my car up and sped away. But as I passed the black sedan, I spotted something out of the corner of my eye—a bumper sticker. I slowed down a little and squinted. My stomach sinking, I realized I had seen it before—many times. In fact, I had an identical sticker on my back bumper.

It read: *My kid is an honors student at Laurelmont High.*

Later in the afternoon, Jamie sat beside me at my outdoor picnic table. Across the low flowerbeds that bordered the eastern edge of the yard, our V-shaped view of Los Angeles peeped through the hills at us.

Still my friend after twenty years, Jamie had dropped everything in response to my emergency phone call.

We were both still in work clothes—in my case, a grubby, clay-spotted apron over shorts and a T-shirt. My friend put me to shame with her black skinny jeans with black patent loafers, a silk blouse, and a blazer. Her long strawberry-blonde hair was up in its trademark ponytail.

"Stay for dinner." I had picked irises from the garden and began to arrange them one by one in a vase.

"Can't," she said. "But I wanted to get your letter to you. I made some revisions, but remember, I'm not a lawyer."

"You're the closest thing I've got to one."

Jamie had been a paralegal and now wrote episodes for the hit TV show *Legal Eagles.*

Rooming together for three years, she and I had become friends more through proximity than through any real similarities in personality or outlook. The fact that we shared everything, including our different reactions to the events around us, had somehow added to the experience of marching together into so-called adulthood.

During our years as roomies, I tolerated her nightly clarinet practice, while she put up with the huge vats of smelly dye I used in my booming college tie-dying business. We dabbled in drugs, trekked the Inca Trail to Machu Picchu, and slept around in numbers we felt qualified us to make generalizations about men and their peculiar ways.

Moreover, Jamie had been with me the days I met both Mike and Brady, and had gotten a front-row seat for those debacles. She advised me when Mike, after four months of dating and lovemaking, started arriving late or canceling dates at the last minute.

"He's going squirrely on you. It's classic male behavior when they're feeling conflicted." She sniffed.

Jamie also held my hand through the far-worse Brady period, when courtship, marriage, pregnancy, birth, separation, and divorce all took place in the course of four short years. Jamie had been with me that night at McHenry's when I met Brady, with his sexy gravelly voice and those blue eyes that lingered over you as if no one in the world could be more interesting or beautiful. She'd given me a thumbs-up and taken a cab home alone when it became clear he was smitten with me, imploring me to stay.

Three months later, Jamie attended our small, impulsively scheduled wedding. After we married, she had shored me up as Brady transitioned from an ardent, charming lover into someone angry, cutting, and sarcastic, who picked me apart in a dozen ways while I struggled to understand why.

"This is all his problem," Jamie opined. "The guy's a nutcase, and the only thing wrong with you is that you stay with him."

Jamie was the sort who thrived on drama, who liked to swoop in and pull you from the brink of disaster. When things were calm, we had less to talk about. It made sense that, when the Daniela problem arose, Jamie was the person I'd called.

"Draft a letter to the parents," she had said, "and let me review it."

"Why?"

"To cover your ass."

"Got it." We didn't learn this stuff in art school. I'd had to spend part of the day drafting the letter and getting Jamie to review it instead of working on the concept for my mural.

She pulled a sheet of paper from a folder and handed it to me. "See what you think of this revision."

Dear Mr. and Mrs. Harris,

After numerous unsuccessful attempts to reach you by phone or text, I am writing you this letter. My son Justin is a junior at Laurelmont High School and a classmate of your daughter Daniela. Two days ago, Daniela accompanied my son home from school, saying she was unable to return to her own home. She claimed to have nowhere else to go. Given no information to substantiate or refute what she's told me, I am, unless I hear otherwise from you, allowing her to stay with me for now. She is safe, and I'm prepared to assist you in keeping her that way. Please feel free to contact her or me whenever it is convenient for you.

Sincerely,
Nicole Adams

"I think you've covered your bases here," Jamie said. "You've disclosed where she is and indicated your willingness to cooperate with them. At the same time, you're not pressuring them to come for her."

"Okay." A nervous queasiness had settled into my stomach. Didn't I have enough problems already as a single mother and sole breadwinner of my little family? "Should I go to their school, maybe tell the principal?"

Jamie thought about it. "We wrote an episode once about a runaway kid. The schools are required by law to report to child services any kid they feel is at risk. If they reported Daniela, she could end up in foster care."

"You're kidding!" I'd heard the stories of abuse and neglect; there was no way I would do that to Daniela.

Or the baby, a tiny voice reminded me.

Jamie took the vase I'd been filling and placed it in the center of the table, my white irises glowing in the twinkle lights above them. "The other thing is, you have to be her legal guardian to do anything for her, like deal with her school or take her to a doctor."

"What? She has to go to the doctor!" This was crazy. I had all the responsibility, with no authority to make decisions or take action. It was a nightmare, worse than I could ever have imagined.

Jamie's eyes filled with sympathy. "Lemme look into it for you."

Caroline appeared beside us, margarita pitcher in hand. "Anyone?" She began to pour out drinks while I tried to put my thoughts into boxes. But I couldn't stop thinking about Daniela. "What if her parents want to have me arrested for kidnapping?"

"That's why you send the letter," Jamie said. "So everyone knows where she is and what your intentions are."

"What if she has the baby and never leaves?"

No one answered. Apparently, nobody was willing to touch that one.

Chapter 12

Mike and I didn't talk during his brief work trip, so when he returned, he knew nothing of what had happened in his absence. I had told Justin that he had to be the one to tell Mike about Daniela's pregnancy.

"He's going to find out, after all, and it should be from you."

One reason I'd been able to stay friends with Mike is that he had never mistreated me or made me feel bad about myself. I was almost painfully eager to see him again, even after just a few days. By the time of his expected arrival, I was hanging out in the car park, which afforded a convenient view of the Trail of Terror winding up the mountain. Sure enough, there was Mike's Jeep on its way up.

He wore a cotton plaid shirt and three days of stubble, his cheeks reddened by the sun. I was so happy to see him that when I ran up to him for a hug, I couldn't stop in time. I collided into his chest with an *oomph.* "Oh, sorry . . . I'm so glad you're back!" Rattled, I pulled away from him. "Justin and I need to talk to you. Right now."

"O . . . kay," he said, his hand lingering on the small of my back. His eyes, which a moment before had been dead tired, now held interest and more than a little concern.

"Don't move. I'll go get Justin. *Justin!*" I screamed, running back through the yard toward the house.

When I returned, pulling my wary, reluctant son behind me, we found Mike at the little table with chairs and an umbrella that I'd put on a spot of nearby grass some years ago. I didn't care that it was next to the car park; the view was pretty and it conveniently allowed you to spy on arriving guests.

Mike had settled himself in. Eyebrows raised, arms crossed over his chest, his whole attitude said, *I'm waiting.*

"Seriously, Mom? You're gonna stay for this?" Justin said as I sat down next to Mike. "This is a man-to-man conversation."

"No. It's a man-to-man-to-Mom conversation."

"Mike!" Justin protested.

He gave Justin an affectionate cuff on the shoulder. "Do what your mother says."

Justin sighed as if he were carrying the weight of the entire planet on his back. It was probably how he really felt too. I flashed on an image of my little boy, two years old, laughing and joyous, running back and forth across our yard with Wolfgang, then a twelve-week-old puppy, indefatigable until . . . BOOM! He had crawled into my arms and was asleep a second later, his sweet head on my shoulder. The sound of his baby breathing was so incredibly delicious.

Tears stung my eyes. My baby was in trouble now.

Meanwhile, he had begun to talk to Mike. "So, you remember that girl I told you about?"

In an instant, the earth stopped spinning. He had told Mike about Daniela?

"Yeah?" Mike said.

Omigod. Mike had known about Daniela, and he hadn't told me. I began to quietly have a coronary.

Justin kept talking. "Well, things with her got kind of, um, intense." He cleared his throat as if in pain.

Mike's calm voice. "Intense?"

"Well, um . . ." Justin made a strangling noise.

"Did you do the deed?"

"The deed?" Justin hunched his shoulders, flushing.

"In other words, did you put it in all the way and keep it in?" Mike certainly had a way of clarifying things.

Justin nodded, his cheeks scarlet.

Mike continued, implacable. "How many times?"

"Twice. In one afternoon."

"Did you use those condoms?"

"Yes! Both times!"

Wait a minute. Did he say *those condoms*? Mike had talked to my son about *condoms?*

"So . . ." Mike's voice was now tinged with regret, as if he was sorry to have to go to this place. "I assume there's a reason you've brought all this up." His eyes met mine in shared dismay.

"She's pregnant." Justin's tone was flat, his face expressionless.

Mike nodded somberly.

I put my hand on Justin's. Sitting there with his head bowed, he looked so defeated and miserable that it was hard to be angry with him. Right now, I found it much easier to be angry with Mike. "Honey." I gritted my teeth. "I need to talk to Mike for a while now."

"Kay." Justin bolted.

We sat there for a minute, Mike looking resigned but unapologetic. "Go ahead," he said. "Say it."

"You knew about Daniela and you *didn't tell me*?" I was up on my feet, pacing and flinging my arms around.

"That's about the size of it."

"Why?"

Mike stood up too. By unspoken agreement, we started to walk down the road toward Stefan's house. "Look, Nic, he came to me. He said he needed a guy to talk to, and he made me promise not to tell you."

"So what? You can't keep a promise like that. You should have told me anyway."

"If I did that, he'd never trust me again. And he'd have no one to talk to."

"What did he say to you, exactly?"

"He'd begun fooling around with this girl. It was obvious where he was headed with it."

"So you gave him condoms? How could you do that?"

"He already had condoms. This brand that I know for a fact is for shit." Mike stopped and turned to face me. "He's almost seventeen, Nicole. He was going to get laid no matter what anyone said."

"So you gave him . . . what? Better condoms?" I tried to keep the sarcasm from my voice.

"Yes, Nicole," Mike said patiently. "Better condoms."

"Yeah, they did a lot of good!"

Mike ran his hand through his hair, looking baffled. "See, that's what I don't get. Those things work. Maybe Justin didn't use them right."

"Or *maybe* the condom broke. It happens, *as you are aware*." There was nothing Mike didn't know about me, including the facts of Justin's conception.

"Normally, when a condom breaks, you know it."

"You *don't* always know it."

Memories of a livid Brady swam into my mind: *"You're lying. You've been cheating on me!"*

"What happened to you was really unusual," Mike said. A corner of his mouth quirked up. "Maybe your condom didn't break. Justin's always been a good swimmer. Maybe his kid is too, for that matter."

"Hah!" I poked him in the ribs, and he poked me back.

We walked for a moment in silence.

"Nic, I'm sorry about keeping that secret from you," Mike said. "Believe me, I lost sleep over it. But I thought when you heard the whole story, you'd understand."

"You thought I'd never find out."

"Yeah, that too."

We both laughed, although not a lot.

It was that beautiful time of day when the sun was going down and the air had a pearly quality and a certain stillness that I'd always loved. As we walked, Mike's hand brushed mine accidentally. I resisted my sudden urge to grab it and hold on.

Then I said, "Oh, by the way, Caroline moved in with me."

"They'll work it out," he said. "I have faith in those two." After a moment, he went on. "So. This girl's pregnant. Now what happens?"

"I guess I have to meet with her parents, although they're horrible, and I think the dad's got a drinking problem." I told Mike everything I knew about them.

"I'll go with you," he said.

"Thanks." I gratefully accepted his offer. If I had to meet with these people, I could use the company of a guy who bench-pressed two hundred fifty pounds.

We turned and started back up the hill. The sun was slipping past the top of the mountains, the sky turning pink.

I sighed. "Justin used to tell me everything. He used to do what I wanted him to."

"Yeah, those days are over. Just be glad you got as much out of him as you did." As we arrived back to the car park, he added, "You and I need to go for a drive soon. We'll go pay Daniela's parents a visit."

Chapter 13

For our first date, Mike and I had shared a steaming bowl of bouillabaisse at a little place in Santa Monica, then got ice-cream cones and walked on the path along the bluffs, overlooking the ocean and talking. Everything was better when you were falling in love—the breeze cooler, the air more fragrant. Hopefulness and contentment bubbled up in my chest.

Mike took my hand, which thrilled me. *He must like me at least a little bit.* I listened to him talk about his job as a film production assistant, while impressions drifted by me. His fingers against mine, the warmth of the sun, the envious glance of a passing girl. His eyes, which scanned the horizon, then turned to meet mine. His lips, which had become objects of fascination. And desire.

He drew me toward a spot overlooking the beach and ocean. "So, anyway, I've decided to try stunt work," he said, stopping and looking down at me. His hand, still holding mine, moved behind his back, pulling me closer to him.

"Isn't that dangerous?" I stared at his lips, only inches away.

He shrugged easily, grinning down at me. "Not if you're careful. It's fun, and the best thing is, you get to travel all the time."

I should have seen the warning signs right then. "Is that what you want, to travel all the time?"

"You know where I spent the first twenty years of my life?" he asked, his voice edged with frustration. "Blythe, California! That'll give you a hunger to go see the world, if nothing will."

I had passed by Blythe a few times along the parched I-10 freeway that traversed the Sonoran Desert, halfway between Los Angeles and Phoenix. "So what's next then?"

"A job that takes me places, shows me things. I can't afford to go anywhere on my own dime."

As I looked back on it, he couldn't have been any clearer.

I nestled my face in his chest, while his hand cupped the back of my head. I was already halfway in love with him when we shared our first kiss, overlooking the ocean, our arms pulling each other close. By the time we'd gone back to my apartment, engaged in slow, steamy foreplay and made love in both the bed and the shower, then downed a breakfast of omelets and fresh-squeezed orange juice, I was officially a goner, besotted.

And so was he.

We did the standard young-people-in-love thing, together every moment, copulating with the frequency of small furry animals, sharing our food, finishing each other's sentences, and it was spectacular. Until the day it wasn't.

Later, when I got perspective on it, I realized that Mike had simply gotten spooked.

That's when he had said it. "Nic, I really, really like you."

He *liked* me? What about all the declarations of undying love?

At least he looked as miserable as I felt.

"Don't call me. Don't come near me," I sobbed.

"But . . . don't leave yet!" His eyebrows drew together.

"I'll leave whenever I want!"

And I did. Mike stayed away from me for a few months, but then crept back, determined to keep me in his life as a friend, calling me every time he returned from a job in Thailand or Denmark or Peru. Soon enough, I was with Brady and had reluctantly placed the memories of Mike, the lover, in boxes in the deep storage corner of my brain.

Mike, the friend, pulled his Jeep up behind a blue Hyundai parked in front of the Harrises' house. The place was unchanged from my last visit, except that the gravel had been stirred around so that dark patches of dirt shone through in some places. I swallowed hard. We hadn't called in advance or been invited, and, from what I knew, I couldn't imagine getting a warm welcome from these people.

The house looked even creepier at night. Its windows, the only dark ones on the block, seemed to follow us like eyes.

Mike looked the house over with skepticism. "Daniela lives here?"

"Afraid so." I wondered who might be peering out at us through the Venetian blinds. Also that blue Hyundai. Surely, that was the blue car I'd seen on our road the other day, the one the dogs were chasing.

"We'll be fine," Mike reassured me, his eyes moving over the house and street as he spoke. We picked our way across the gravel toward the front door, where he punched the doorbell, a glittering pink jewel embedded in swirling white plastic.

The sound of movement inside. Then footsteps coming toward us and stopping near the door. But it didn't open. The person was standing on the other side, listening.

Prickles ran up and down my neck.

Mike knocked on the door. "Anyone there? We'd like to talk to you about your daughter Daniela."

After a moment, with interminable slowness, the dead bolt slid open. My skin was crawling, and my heart was pounding. I slipped my arm through Mike's and pressed against his side.

"It's okay," he whispered, giving me a nod.

The door opened. A woman stood there, small, clearly Daniela's mother. The same dark hair and eyes. The same slender build. She wore a dark-gray, long-sleeved turtleneck and black pants, tailored and perfectly fitting. Her hair was pulled back into a French braid at the nape of her neck, while a simple, heavy gold bracelet encircled her wrist.

The austere, elegant clothes matched her expression; neither matched the garish pink house. That house was the last place I would have imagined this person to live. Or Daniela, for that matter.

"Why do you speak of my daughter?" She had a slight foreign accent, which probably explained the odd formality of her speech. Daniela had told me that, while her father was American, her mother was from Chile, and that she'd grown up speaking Spanish at home.

"I'm Nicole Adams. Daniela is staying with me." I gave her the biggest smile I could muster.

The hard lines in her face grew softer. "Tell me, please, how is my daughter? But hurry! We have only a few moments before . . ."

Before what? A car came around the corner, its headlights illuminating her front yard. The woman flinched. As the car passed on, she quivered with tension, speaking in a tightly controlled voice. "Come inside!"

Looking back over her shoulder toward the street, she pulled us through the door and dead bolted it.

In the center of the living room stood a cheap-looking orange-and-gold sofa and a couple of gold armchairs, all of which screamed *rental furniture.* No photos, knickknacks, or anything personal. Opened half-empty boxes occupied the corners of the room, as if someone had moved in and only partially unpacked. A folded ironing board leaned against one wall. A sewing machine case sat on the floor.

How long had they lived here? Daniela had said she'd been at Laurelmont since September. Eight months.

The woman lowered her voice. "It will not be safe for you if . . .

anyone arrives. We will stay here and talk, while I watch for cars. When I see one, I will take you to the back door, and you will go out immediately and walk along the side of our house to your car. Am I clear?"

"We can help you," Mike started in.

"If anyone sees you here, I fear that things will become very, very difficult."

"But—"

"For the love of God, please! Listen and do as I say!"

"We will." My heart had gone out to this woman, whose problems apparently dwarfed my own by a landslide. "But why haven't you returned my calls?"

The woman's face grew pinched and tight. "My daughter is safe with you. Promise me. No one must know where she is."

"She is totally safe. Who are you afraid of—her father?" I asked.

"Does he know where she's living?" Mike asked.

Dry-eyed, she faced us, her hands balling into fists. "No, and he must never learn."

A shiver passed through me. No wonder Daniela wanted to stay with us. "But the letter I sent you . . . ?"

"I took it from the mailbox. He never saw it."

"Why is he angry? Is it the pregnancy?"

Her grim silence was my answer.

"Is he trying to find her?" Mike asked.

She shook her head. "In this moment, he is done with her." Her lips tightened and her eyes darkened. "It must remain like this. He must not be reminded. He must not become angry with her again."

"So you left her at school?" I ventured.

"I took Daniela to school and told her to find a kind family to help her. I was frightened, and it was all I could think of to do."

"But you want her back?"

Her lips trembled. "I want her protected. Right now, she is safe."

The sounds of a car engine and the flash of headlights interrupted us. She jumped, a hand to her throat. "Come with me!" She pulled us down a hallway toward the back of the house.

I could feel resistance rippling through Mike. Running away would not have been his solution to the problem. At the same time, he didn't pick unnecessary fights. Reluctantly, he followed us.

We reached the back door.

"Now, go! Walk to the right and then very quietly down the side of the house to the street. I will distract him inside."

"We can't leave you here with him," I said at the same time that Mike said, "Come with us."

"I will stay. It is for the best."

The sound of a key in the lock.

I grabbed Mike's hand and we slipped out into the dark. A man's voice sounded, but I couldn't make out words. Mike had turned into a stone statue, refusing to move, listening intently. I pulled on his hand. "Come on!" I kept my voice low, worried the guy inside would hear us.

"I can't leave her," he whispered.

"Let's go along the side and try to hear something."

The good part was these people did not invest in exterior lighting. We crept along unobserved, staying below window level and stopping to listen. The bad part was the gravel everywhere, which crunched under our feet and caused me to slide and lose my footing. Only Mike's steadying arm kept me on my feet; still, I was sure the man at this very moment was putting us in his gun sights.

"This may be a bedroom," Mike whispered, laying a finger on his lips. We squatted below the windows until, sure enough, a light came on just above us. I recognized Daniela's mother as a soft murmur, while the man's voice was louder, allowing me to catch a word or phrase. "Shitty day . . . brat. . . for her own good."

Then, more low murmurs, tinkling laughter, and the light went off. After a minute, Mike gestured to me and we slipped back to the car. Once safely locked inside, I shuddered and allowed myself to moan about how little we'd accomplished. "I didn't get any of Daniela's things or work out any kind of solution."

"I don't think a lot of rational solutions get worked out in that house."

The thought kept going through my head: If Daniela's dad came to get her, what could I do? How could I protect her?

It terrified me that I didn't have an answer for that.

Chapter 14

Pruning shears in hand, I was waging war on the bougainvillea, which had engulfed its trellis and taken over its corner of the yard.

Caroline perched on the edge of a nearby chaise with her glass of lemonade. She would be starting dinner soon. "Where's Mike tonight?" she asked.

I whacked off a branch. "I think he has a date."

Her nose wrinkling, she made a *tsk* sound with her tongue. "And you're okay with that?"

"Why wouldn't I be?" I stopped clipping for a moment to look at her.

"Nicki! Seriously?"

I tried to think how to explain Mike to my sister, a woman who'd spent all of her adult life with the same man. In this day and age, Caroline was a true innocent.

"He usually has a woman or two that he . . . sees, you know. Nothing serious." I'd heard names—Joni, Maria, Paige—and some lasted longer than others, but in the end, they all went in and out the revolving door.

"Really? You always say he's the best man you know."

"He is. He has the right to see other women. He and I are just friends." I could understand how it would seem strange to Caroline.

"I'm sure Grant has never slept with anyone but me."

"Oh, please. That's just weird."

"It is not! We've always been enough for each other." Her scowl and the fierce set of her shoulders conveyed how sincere she was. "We still are."

How could she say that when he'd left her? I thought it but didn't speak the words aloud.

She understood me anyway. "Nicki, we've never fought or disagreed on anything. We never cheated or fell out of love."

"But you're separated."

"That's just because Grant lost himself when he lost his business. I keep praying that, when he finds himself again, he'll find me too."

The second and last time that Brady saw Justin was by accident, just before his first birthday. He hadn't come for the purpose of visiting his son, but rather to sign divorce papers and unload the two of us for good. At the time this happened, Mike was in Africa, teaching.

Grant, who had taken on the role of my protective big brother when he married Caroline, felt I shouldn't be alone when Brady came by. He insisted on being present. A two-time state spelling bee champion, winner of multiple science awards, and finalist in a national debate competition, my brother-in-law was a powerhouse.

Intellectually.

That being said, it made me smile to think of Grant as my bodyguard. Although his confidence and perfect posture made him seem bigger than he was, he probably tipped the scales at a hundred and fifty pounds. If it came down to a physical confrontation with Brady, or really anyone else, I'd give myself better odds than I would Grant. I had at least taken a class in self-defense and knew which sensitive areas to jab. Nonetheless, I was happy for the moral support.

Of course, Caroline came along also.

When Brady arrived, my sister and Grant were seated in my

breakfast nook on either side of Justin's high chair. They were attempting to get food into their godson.

They'd said from the beginning that they wanted kids but had never actually had any. Personally, knowing firsthand about the needs of small children, I didn't think this was so bad. Grant and Caroline enjoyed a kind of togetherness so effortless and so absolute that it sometimes felt there was no room around them for anyone else. In the middle of a group discussion, they were known for falling into a conversation of their own from which they wouldn't emerge, content to spend the whole evening talking and laughing with each other. I wasn't sure their little household could accommodate a third person, not even a beloved child.

Grant and Caroline had read some baby books and were trying to apply what they'd learned. Unfortunately, Justin had not read the same books they had.

"Here comes the choo-choo train!" Grant sang, advancing a spoonful of avocado steadily in Justin's direction. "Open up for the choo-choo train!" A lock of his dark hair fell down between his eyebrows as he concentrated.

"Whoo whoooo!" Caroline mimicked a train whistle.

At age zero, Justin was already his own person. He fed himself with his own hands, thank you very much, and would not sit still and open his mouth for an advancing train or spoon, no matter what was on it. My little boy had also recently discovered that it was more fun to throw food than eat it.

He grabbed the spoon from Grant just as Brady strolled into my kitchen looking tanned, pleased with himself, but annoyed to be wasting his time with this nonsense.

"Gaaah!" Justin crowed, flinging the spoon into the air, and catapulting mashed avocado onto my soon-to-be ex-husband's khaki pants.

"Fffff—" Brady stopped himself before uttering the expletive—for him, a supreme act of self-control.

He gave the barest glance to Justin, who, wearing nothing but a diaper, sat cherubic and platinum-curled in his high chair. Blobs of macaroni and cheese, along with avocado, clung to his cheeks and shoulders, to Caroline's hair, and to the tassels on Grant's loafers.

"The papers," Brady said.

I handed them over, trying not to speak or look at him directly. The mere sight of my husband made me panicky, my stomach flipping over, a bad taste in my mouth.

It took but a few seconds for him to sign and begin making tracks for the door. He raised a hand to a stony-faced Grant and Caroline, shot a last glance toward Justin, then me. Something about the look on my face seemed to stop him cold. His expression changed and, for a moment, I saw a bit of the Brady I'd first met, the attentive, charming man who had loved me.

My heart twisted at the thought of what could have been. Or at least, what I had thought could have been. But Brady had not truly been the person he appeared to be at first. I'd been fooled.

"Be well," Brady said.

"Oh, I will." I turned away from him as he left. As much as I was glad to be rid of him and to have survived this part of my life, I found myself feeling drained and miserable. "Let's go sit in the living room."

I plucked Justin from his high chair, swabbed off most of the chunks with a wet paper towel, and sat on the sofa with my child in my lap, playing with his toes. "This little piggy went to market. This little piggy stayed home."

Justin laughed that wonderful baby laugh and kicked his feet. He twisted around to see me and put his sticky hands on my face. "Mama," he said. His first word.

"Omigod, did you hear that? Justin just said Mama!"

"He did! He did say Mama!" Caroline was almost as excited as I was.

She and Grant began to debate whether it was unusually early for a boy to say his first word at fewer than twelve months and whether or not that meant Justin was a genius. I didn't care. All I cared about was that his first word had been my name.

I took it as a sign, a sign that it was just him and me, against the world. I had a special bond with my boy, I knew it. A bond that would never be broken.

But now, sixteen years later, I wondered if I'd been fooled again. Not by Brady, but this time by my son, my little boy, with whom I'd once felt so close.

Chapter 15

I drove Bernice down the Trail of Terror, my foot riding the brake as usual, my front teeth biting my lower lip. I'd never been a speed demon on this road, but especially not on delivery day when I loaded my car with meticulously wrapped and packed ceramics pieces and brought them to my nearby post office for shipment all over the world. This day's load included the table service for eight, which was a wedding gift going to Santa Fe, New Mexico; a half dozen twenty-four-inch vases for a boutique hotel in Vermont; and various pieces commissioned by individuals—decorative bowls, plaques, and platters.

I was approaching Stefan's house when I saw him out on the road walking Wolfgang. He was in his fifties, squat with bits of frizz around his ears, a grin full of blindingly white, oversize purchased teeth, and, I'd been told, one of the most demonic imaginations in Hollywood. I didn't enjoy horror myself, so I was not familiar with Stefan's body of work, but his films made hundreds of millions of dollars.

Although he was originally from Germany, his English was the perfect product of British boarding schools. "Hello, Nicole. Are you off to post your pots?"

"I am. How are you and Wolfgang?"

Stefan cocked his head toward a little sedan parked on the pullout next to his mailbox. I hadn't paid attention because there were often cars down here belonging to his visitors.

"I'm about to go speak to the person in that blue Hyundai. It was parked here yesterday, and I cannot imagine any reason for it being here a second day."

Blue Hyundai? Was it the car I'd seen in front of Daniela's

house? I squinted at the windshield but saw only the outline of a person—a woman, if the poufy hair was any indication.

I stared. Daniela's mother? The driver must have already noticed us looking her way, because she started the car, made a hasty U-turn, then sped off down the road.

Follow it.

Yeah, right. Even at my most adventurous, espionage had never been part of my bag of tricks. And yet . . .

"Stefan, I gotta run, okay?"

"Nicole, wait!"

I rolled down my window as he anxiously motioned to me.

"You'll take Wolfgang next week, remember, when my shoot starts in Vermont?"

"I'm planning on it!" Wolfgang would be with me a lot this summer, while Stefan crisscrossed the country. "See you soon!"

I gunned it forward as fast as one could with a thousand pounds of ceramics in their car, but by now the Hyundai was long gone. I drove all the way down Laurel Canyon, then cruised Hollywood and Sunset Boulevards until I noticed the needle of my gas gauge scraping the bottom of the red zone.

Maybe the woman in the blue car had been the mother. Maybe she just wanted to see her kid and make sure she was safe. In her shoes, I would have done it.

Maybe this woman grieved for her daughter as I did for my son, his college and career to be replaced by diapers and night school, girlfriends and prom night giving way to custody and child support.

Maybe my sweet kid had been replaced by a lost soul, a young man in so far over his head that he would never see the sky again. I couldn't bear it.

Soon, my entire life would be a box labeled Saving Justin.

These days, in our crowded house, it was a challenge to get Justin alone for two minutes of private conversation.

While Daniela was in the yard with the dogs, I caught him coming out of the bathroom, still wet from the shower, shirtless, a towel tied around his waist. The broadened shoulders, the hair on his chest—how had I failed to realize he was now more a man than a boy, no longer the skinny tadpole I'd raised? I couldn't bring myself to look at him.

"I want to take Daniela out on Saturday for a little one-on-one. You know, lunch, manicure. Girl stuff."

He regarded me with surprise. "Why?"

"To get to know her. Find out how she's feeling about things."

"Okay." He shrugged. "Actually, that's good, 'cause I've got that SAT prep class."

"That's this Saturday?"

Like all the other junior class parents, I was getting caught up in the madness, enrolling Justin in ridiculously expensive prep classes for the entrance exams to universities with ridiculously high tuitions. A horrible thought occurred to me.

"Is Daniela taking that?"

"No idea."

Was I supposed to be responsible for that too? Her academic prospects, her extracurricular activities? I began to hyperventilate. An unfamiliar fear gripped me. I'd never before been afraid of the future.

Focus.

He turned as if about to leave, then wavered. Not wanting to end this rare moment of time alone with him, I quickly said, "Is there anything you want to ask me . . . or tell me?"

A haunted look came over his face. “Mom, I don’t have to marry her, do I?”

“Of course not!”

“What about when the baby comes?” His voice rose in panic. “Do I have to coach her? At the hospital? I don’t want to!” His voice rose even higher.

I forced myself to think. “The mother chooses someone she’s comfortable with. In this case, I think Daniela would want her mother.”

Justin sagged with relief. “Yeah, that’d be good.”

I heard footsteps outside, Daniela’s voice approaching as she called to the dogs. The sound of the screen door opening.

“We don’t have to decide all that right now,” I said. “Just deal with today.”

That’s what I was doing. It was all any of us could do.

Chapter 16

So swift was my passage through marriage that I was already divorced and a mother by the time Mike got back from his volunteer time in Africa. He looked me up a week after his return.

"It's been a long time," he said. "We should get together and swap stories."

"Well, since I have a baby now, most of my stories aren't that interesting."

"Try me," he said.

It turned out that Mike didn't mind the realities of parenting a small child. He was always willing to bring me children's Tylenol when Justin had a fever, to lug around not only a baby but also all the related accessories, to make a quick exit from places where Justin could not keep quiet. I wondered about his intentions sometimes, but the fact was, he was always dating someone else and wasn't shy about mentioning it.

I did believe in his friendship, though. He always made time for Justin and me.

When my son was four, and December came around gray, rainy, and depressing, I couldn't imagine rallying my energy to put on a proper Christmas for him.

"Mike!" I suggested. "Let's take Justin and drive up to Mammoth. We'll have a real white Christmas, with snow."

We rented a house and the three of us drove up on the twenty-third.

Caroline had given me Justin's Christmas present early: a pricy red snowsuit with shiny red boots and a multicolored striped scarf and a hat. The jacket bore little embroidered trains on the pockets and required dry cleaning. I hung the precious thing carefully away and packed the warm, practical jacket I'd got from the lost and found at his private preschool, where all the abandoned rich-kid belongings went to die.

For myself, I brought leggings under jeans, some old hiking boots, and a down parka that had been Caroline's in high school.

We arrived at the foreign winter wonderland of Mammoth early in the afternoon, Justin's face pressed to the car window as he stared out at the cold white stuff he'd only seen on television. We bundled up in a hurry and rushed from our cabin into the frosty air.

"Look, Justin, snow! Look at those icicles hanging down."

"Snow!" he shouted, running over to a big bank of it and plunging his hands in up to the elbow. A minute later, he had torn off his gloves, while I scrambled to retrieve them, and was scooping the stuff with his bare hands. "It's cold, Mommy!"

"It sure is." I threw a snowball at him, which made him yell happily and throw one back at me. Soon, the three of us were pelting each other.

Mike and I were both laughing at Justin's excitement. My eyes met his. "Have you ever done this?" I asked.

He shook his head, while we looked at each other in wonderment, realizing that, although we'd both seen snow, neither of us two southern California rats had ever played in it as children. Like Justin, we were doing this for the first time.

Mike packed snow into his fist and approached me with an evil grin.

"Forget it." I pointed a finger at him. "No!" I shrieked, running away as fast as I could in knee-high snow.

He bombarded me with a couple of snowballs in quick succession, while Justin hurled himself between us, shouting.

"Let's get him!" I yelled to Justin, and we both turned on Mike, abandoning snowball-making to simply tackle him and throw him into a snowbank. I gained a quick advantage by tucking a handful of snow down Mike's shirt collar, my hands smarting from the icy crystals. With a roar, he managed to jump to his feet, but Justin clamped onto his leg like a barnacle.

"Take him down!" I screamed, flinging snow.

"Aaagh, ya got me!" Mike pretended to crumple. "Aargh, stop, stop, I surrender!" He lay on the ground in defeat, while I dogpiled on top of them. Just as quickly, Justin wiggled out, did a victory dance around us, then ran off, whooping.

For a brief second, I lay there flashing back to another time when I had lain atop Mike, feeling his hot skin and his breath on my face. I could tell by his sudden stillness that he remembered it too. We lay there for a moment, our lips just a few inches apart, until a warning bell began to ring in my head.

Nothing but trouble . . .

I slowly rolled away and squatted beside Mike, who uttered a few fake groans of pain. Pretending to inspect his wounds, I whispered in his ear, "You don't have to let him win every time, you know. Soon enough, he'll be beating you for real."

Justin was now ten yards away, digging under a bush with a stick. The crisp, cold air had painted spots of red on his cheeks; his breath emerged in white puffs. "Look, Mom!" He breathed ecstatically and pointed.

"Yeah. I should probably take a few wins now, while I still can." Mike grinned at me as he rose to his feet.

We walked along until we came to a spectacular row of icicles hanging from the sloped bottom edge of a rooftop. Mike picked up Justin, holding him in the crook of one arm, and reaching out the other arm to snap off an icicle. "They're kind of like nature's Popsicles." He licked the icicle, then passed it to my boy, who happily received it.

Reaching a snowbank near our cabin, all three of us lay down to make angels, then retreated inside. Mike made a fire while I put

Justin down for a nap. It took no time, as my little boy was practically asleep on his feet. He would be down for a good two hours.

When I emerged from the bedroom, Mike was kneeling before the fireplace, gently blowing to ignite some dry kindling, then tending to the tiny flame until the log above it caught fire. For just a moment, looking at his cupped hands and the fine hair on his wrists and forearms, I allowed myself to go back in time, to imagine and regret the loss of what might have been. We could have been lovers, soul mates, parents together . . .

Mike looked over and caught me staring at him. "What?" His tone was good-natured but curious, as if he'd seen a strange look on my face.

My throat dry and scratchy, I moved into the kitchen and called out, "Beer or hot chocolate?"

"Beer."

"Scrabble or poker?"

"Poker."

By the time we sat down at the big table to play, I was myself again, unflappable and self-contained. "Better watch out. My luck's running hot these days!"

"Ooh, I'm afraid!"

"Be afraid. Be very afraid." Giving Mike a knowing look, I shuffled and dealt the cards.

Chapter 17

Daniela and I had gotten our mani-pedis and now sat at a little table in the window of Turnip, a vegan restaurant in Los Feliz. My elbows rested on a yellow gingham tablecloth next to a trio of daisies in a bud vase.

I couldn't believe she'd only been with us a week. It felt like a year since the kids had made their announcement.

A girl in her twenties approached. "Would you like to hear our Question of the Day?" She rolled on even as I opened my mouth to say no. "*What action can you take today for a better tomorrow?*"

"Um, lovely. We'll need a few minutes." I said it as nicely as I could; I didn't want to sound as irritated and worried as I felt.

"Let me know when you're ready!"

I waited until she was out of earshot. "Go on," I said to Daniela, who sat holding the menu she'd not yet opened.

I tried to picture how it had been for her, left at school like an unwanted shoe in the lost and found, abandoned for someone else to take home. She must have been so scared.

"I was going to ask my friend Heather to take me, but her mom wouldn't have liked it." Daniela picked up her fork and played with it. "I thought of you because Justin's friends say you're super cool and really nice to them."

"They do?" I loved Justin's friends. Charlie with his long, serious face and funny laugh, and Amos, who told fart jokes but would probably be the class valedictorian.

"Yeah," Daniela went on. "Amos told me about the time his parents had to go to London for a family emergency, and he ended up staying with you for a month. He said he didn't want to go home."

"We loved having him." I supposed I should have been flattered by Daniela's portrait of me. Hell, I *was* flattered, even though in this case my good hostess reputation had basically served only to bite me in the butt. "Have your folks tried to reach you since you came to us?"

Daniela shook her head. "They're done with me." The same words her mother had used. She took a couple of huge, gasping breaths, as if about to break into sobs, then quickly opened her menu as the server walked up again. After staring at it blankly for a second, she threw it down. "I can't decide!" She dissolved into tears.

"What about the turnip vegan cobb salad? We'll take two," I told the server. Finally, she left.

I cleared my throat. "You know, Mike and I went by your house the other day. We spoke to your mother."

Her eyes grew round. "You should've asked me first." I could see her shutting down before my eyes, her head lowering, her shoulders hunching forward.

I felt like I had to ask. "Daniela, how are things at home for you? Do your parents . . . treat you okay?"

"Sure," she said quickly. "My mom always takes care of me. And my dad's cool . . . most of the time." She bit her lips, picked up her fork, and put it down again. "Except . . . sometimes he drinks too much."

"Has he ever hurt you?"

"No!" She stared at me in alarm. "He just gets really mad, but no. He doesn't hurt me."

I leaned forward. "This is important, Daniela. Does your father behave . . . inappropriately with you? Does he touch you or try to kiss you . . . ?"

Her lips began to tremble. "*No, ew!* He's my dad! No way!" Seeing my face, she gave me a pleading look. "Really, I'm telling you the truth. He's just . . . scary when he drinks."

I fought for composure, struggling to keep my voice even. "So what do you really want, Daniela? Is it to stay with us?" I hated to even say it aloud, as if saying it would make it real, but I also needed to know what I was dealing with.

She lifted her eyes to mine, and with every cell of her body transmitted a silent response: *Yes, please, please, let me stay.* The intensity of her need bowled me over.

The walls were closing in on me. The feeling was oddly bittersweet. "You understand, don't you, that I have no legal right to keep you in my home? If your mom or dad shows up, I have to let you go."

"They won't come for me."

I wasn't so sure. At that moment, our salads arrived. I pushed mine to the side, unable to even look at it. Daniela poked at a lettuce leaf with her fork.

"Daniela, what kind of relationship do you have with Justin . . . these days? Or, what do you expect to have now?" I myself wasn't sure how I felt about this. My first reaction had been, *No sex under my roof,* but these kids were sixteen, not ten. I didn't want to spy on my son and I couldn't keep an eye on him around the clock.

At the same time, when I'd asked him about it, Justin hadn't seemed to foresee even a short-term future with Daniela.

The girl looked at me steadily. "Justin's really great. He's stood by me through all this. He'll be a good dad."

"So, you mainly see yourselves as . . . co-parents?"

She nodded.

Co-parents? What was I doing, talking about co-parenting with Daniela? How on earth had I let her lead me so far down this road, way further than I'd expected?

"Whoa! Hold on, let's back up. This is a huge decision, and you should think through all your choices. Have you . . ." I slowed down as she tensed, her eyebrows drawing together. "Have you considered that you might potentially . . . end the pregnancy, or have the baby and put it up for adoption?" Just saying it brought a heaviness to my heart.

"No!" Daniela half rose in her restaurant chair. "I won't do either one."

The server popped up behind her. She began to ask, "All done?" then noticed our untouched plates. Her mouth fell open.

"Two boxes," I said.

Toward Daniela, I felt a weird mixture of anger and relief. The anger won out. "You don't ask for much, do you? You leave me no choice but to take you and this baby in and raise you and support you."

"But it's your grandchild. Don't you care about that?"

I did. I cared a lot. But it seemed that up until now, I'd managed to hide from myself how thrilled I was about this grandchild, despite the terrible circumstances. I had compressed Justin's baby into a small box and put it far away up high in a corner of my mind.

Because I didn't think having the baby was the best thing for Justin, and I had to put him first.

But for me? A new baby to love, a grandchild? Already I could hear his little voice calling my name. *Nana.* With a huge effort, I put those dangerous thoughts back into their box and stored them away for what I hoped would be a long, long time.

Chapter 18

The next morning, Justin took off in his car and Daniela embarked on teaching Caroline to knit. As for me, I frantically threw pots in the studio. I couldn't concentrate on my mural until I was comfortable that my finances were in order, and it was pretty obvious that any increased income that I might need to support my bigger family would have to come from Clayworks. I tried to calculate in my head how much additional income I would earn from every extra hour of work, but my math skills being what they were, I came up with a different answer every time.

Yesterday's conversation with Daniela had pretty much solidified her place in my home, for the time being, anyway. As for Caroline, she was my sister and owned half of my house. I could never afford to buy her out. My visitors, for now, were staying.

Justin's college expenses, which would only partly be covered by a small inheritance, loomed ahead like a deadly iceberg. My pottery business covered my day-to-day expenses plus whatever monthly savings I could put toward the college fund. However, if my food and household expenses went up, the college savings plan would go out the window, not to mention my hope of leaving dinner plates behind and making real art. I was getting shortness of breath and elbow rashes just thinking about it.

If this thing lasted for more than a few weeks, I would need a strategy and a plan, things I'd never been able to wrap my artist's brain around very well. Fortunately, I had Jamie, my great friend in a crisis.

We conferred that afternoon as we went for a run in her neighborhood of West Hollywood. The physical activity was entirely Jamie's idea. I had protested, but she always got what she wanted. It was Sunday afternoon and the dog walkers were out in force with their dachshunds, chihuahuas, and other tiny apartment dogs, all pitter-pattering along on their tiny apartment dog legs. I preferred the speed of the dog walkers to that of Jamie, who galloped effortlessly while I huffed and puffed behind her.

"Can Daniela call home to get some of her things?" she yelled to me over her shoulder. "You shouldn't have to buy her clothes, after all."

"She's not in touch with them." Out of breath, I stopped talking.

"And can Caroline get a job to help with the expenses?"

"Mmm . . . probably better to give her something to do at home."

Caroline meant well, but her duties had been minimal as so-called office manager for her husband's high-tech business. I had no idea what else she might be qualified to do.

In the six days since she'd moved in, I had quickly come to see how depressed she was, far worse than I'd realized. After organizing every fork, pot, pan, and appliance in my kitchen into descending order by size, she had retreated to her bed in the screened porch, where she lay, headphones on, singing along to music only she could hear.

I would give her some time.

"The other thing," I said, "is I have to carve out some hours every day to work on my museum project. I haven't done a thing, and a week's gone by."

Jamie helped me set out a work schedule for myself and some family rules for discussion at dinner, then kissed me goodbye, saying, "Go forth! Lead your people!"

That night, as Caroline ladled out bowls of chili with cheese and sour cream, I brought the subject up.

Justin sat across from me on the picnic bench, expressionless. Until Daniela had moved in and silenced him, I hadn't realized how much Justin's noise factored into the background of my life. Tuneless songs from the shower, the music from his radio and guitars. The sound of constant, restless movement—doors banging, feet thumping on the wood floors.

More than that, I missed his companionship, the frequent "Mom!" followed by "Guess what I was . . ." or "What do you think about . . . ?" All that had stopped.

Daniela sat next to him, not ignoring him exactly, but not engaging him, either. "Would you pass the salt, Justin?" she asked politely.

He moved it toward her without replying.

Caroline put a bowl of chili in front of me.

I cleared my throat. "Family meeting, folks. We need to agree on a few rules for living together. I'm going to have to spend a lot of extra time in my studio, so I'll need help."

"What kind of rules?" Daniela asked.

"Things like cleaning up after ourselves. Can we all agree that everyone will keep their own area tidy?"

I started to go through my list. During peak usage periods, no person would spend more than ten minutes at a time in our one small bathroom. We would do our own laundry, prepare our own breakfasts and lunches, and clean up our own messes.

They nodded in agreement.

"Caroline, are you up for doing the grocery shopping and cooking dinner every night? We'll rotate the cleanup afterward."

"Yes, of course," she said.

"Caroline and Justin will drive Daniela where she needs to go?" I looked over questioningly at them.

"Fine," Caroline said.

Justin looked up. "What're *you* gonna do, Mom?" His tone held no challenge or snark, more of a mild curiosity, but it was enough to set me off. I flared like a Fourth of July firework.

"Excuse me? What'm I going to do?" I rose halfway off the bench. "You want to hear my schedule? I'll be working in my studio from eight a.m. to six p.m., making my Clayworks pottery, then from seven to eleven p.m. on my mural. I'm gonna be responsible for not one but two teenagers and a new baby as well. I'm responsible for everything that happens here, including everything that goes wrong. Is that good enough for you?"

Dinner continued in silence and ground to an end shortly thereafter. I stalked off to the studio, feeling sorry for myself. I also had a good measure of guilt for dumping my problems out in front of the kids. This was not how a proper adult acted.

I'd always disliked working evenings, but from now on, it couldn't be avoided. I had to put in extra hours to do the museum project. I also had to produce more Clayworks stuff, and I could only do that if I put in more hours. I had designed a line of candlesticks—big robust ones, twelve to twenty-four inches high—that would hold those thick pillar candles. They looked great arranged in groups of three at different heights. I had a trio of prototypes standing on a low table in a corner of my living room, and people always noticed them. I prayed they would want to buy them.

As I set off across the grass, I sensed Daniela right behind me with Wolfgang, who was staying with us. Her dejected eyes and drooping face silently reproached me for my outburst.

"I'm taking him for a walk, if that's okay," she said, pointing down the Trail of Terror and coming to stand in the door of my studio. "Nicole, I'm so sorry. This is so hard for you, and I should have thought about it from your side."

"Honey, *I'm* sorry. You're handling this the best way you can, and so is Justin."

"But a new baby! It's so much work."

"My grandchild," I reminded her. "I think that's worth a little effort."

As I moved around turning on the lights, Daniela, looking relieved, gazed with interest at the big potter's wheel, the shelves of pottery awaiting glazing or shipment.

"How's it going with your mural?"

"It's not." My eyes felt scratchy and I gave a shaky sigh.

"Is it hard to get ideas?"

"Everything's hard." Then, hearing how I sounded, I mentally kicked myself. "But I'll get there."

"You think I could come here sometimes to help out? I have some time now, and I'll have more this summer, after finals end. You know, cleaning up and some of the simple stuff."

"That'd be great," I said, pleased she was interested.

She started to leave, the basset hound at her heels.

"Take a flashlight and remember to keep him close to you," I called out. Night was coming on fast.

"Í will!" She took off, calling the dog to walk beside her.

She is such a sweet girl, I thought. Pleasant and anxious to pull her weight, always offering to help. She was easy to have around. That was one good thing at least.

Chapter 19

For a week, we lived quietly, following our daily rules. I worked on Clayworks pottery in my studio for the ten hours a day that Jamie and I had decided upon. It was soul-crushing. Neither my spirit nor my ceramic pieces was intended for mass production. Even on these commercial pieces, I liked to work slowly, letting a piece take its time, letting the colors and shapes come to me as I went along. I liked having three or four pieces going at the same time at different stages of production. Sometimes, glazing one item gave me ideas for shaping a new piece of clay on the wheel. Or a new design for a pot would give me a concept for a candlestick.

Now I had to spend my time planted at the wheel, banging out fairly similar pieces as fast as I could, followed by more time spent slapping on the glazes. I feared I'd embarked on a giant lose-lose, where, by trying to increase sales, I would in fact lower them by lowering the quality of my work.

The thought of losing my livelihood terrified me. I racked my brain for a solution, but nothing came to me. At the same time, I was struggling to put together this upcoming museum show, which was raising challenges I'd never faced before.

For one thing, I had suddenly realized I couldn't attach the tiles directly onto the museum walls, partly because I had to take them down at the end of the show, and partly because I couldn't spend hours at the museum doing the work. I had to prepare the work in my studio. I would have to make the piece here on a different base, then carry it to the museum and install it.

Also, this thing was heavy. I had to be able to carry it and transport it. It made sense to make the mural in pieces and then assemble them on the museum wall.

Hence, my one accomplishment so far: three plywood rectangles built to fill the nine-by-twelve-foot area of the mural. They would fit together nicely on the wall to form a single piece. I had them propped up in a back corner of my studio—three ugly, empty planks silently reproaching me for my lack of ideas. Those that had flowed so generously during with my meeting with the board had all turned out to be dead ends, impossible to implement or otherwise flawed. Nothing else had come in to replace them. *Patience*, I told myself. *Inspiration will come.*

One bright spot had been Daniela, who, true to her promise, had started coming out to lend a hand. She had a knack for seeing what needed to be done and would pick up a broom and sweep the place clean, then empty the overflowing trash bins without my even having to ask. She had a good hand for glazing and had even done few pieces on her own. "I'll show you how to use the wheel," I promised. "You'll be making your own pots soon!"

Jamie had called me with some encouraging news. "California law allows pregnant teenagers to obtain medical care without the consent of a parent or legal guardian," she reported. "All you have to do is drop her off at the doctor's office."

I breathed a sigh of relief. "Would you like me to take you to Planned Parenthood for an appointment?" I asked Daniela, glad that at least that much would be easy.

"Mom said I was fine and didn't need to go right away."

I remembered the woman was an obstetrical nurse. She would know what was needed. The girl had been with us for only two weeks. "Still, it wouldn't be a bad idea to get you started with prenatal care."

Daniela's face crumpled. "I hate to put you to the trouble. Do you mind if I have Heather take me?"

She needed to do this soon, but I hesitated to push her. She wasn't my daughter.

"It's no trouble, but if that's what you want." I made a mental note to remind her.

Daniela continued taking strolls down the hill in the evening. She and Wolfgang would head off together, walking companionably side by side.

Caroline and Justin performed their household duties without complaint but remained silent and in their own worlds. I grieved for them, especially my little boy—never mind that he was now five-foot-eleven. Part of his discomfort, I realized, was that he'd given up his room to Daniela. I couldn't believe I hadn't thought of this earlier. He had no privacy, no real place for his things, and was reduced to slipping in and out of the room for his stuff whenever he could.

I stood in my studio, wondering what I could do about it. There was a small bathroom in the back and a little room that I used as my office, although increasingly it had become a storage room. Emptied and repainted, it could serve as a small bedroom. Yes, the plumbing was exposed and the overhead lamp was a lightbulb with a string, but it had a window for natural light and a door for privacy. And it would be all his.

Excited, I pulled out my cell and called Justin. "Come to the studio! I want to show you something."

When we walked into the room, I spread my arms out in triumph. "Ta-da!"

"What?" His eyes had that deer-in-the-headlights look that he wore so frequently these days.

"Your new bedroom!" Hope and excitement filled me. "We paint, we put in a bed and Wi-Fi—your own private place!"

He took it in, his face contorted as if he were in pain. His next words came out in a burst of misery, slicing into me. *"Who cares?"*

"What!?"

"I'm completely screwed, Mom!" He took a few ragged breaths, as if he'd been running. "I mean, why does she get to decide everything? This is my life too. She wants to have this baby, so that's it. I have no say."

I had no answer for him. I'd always thought of these decisions as naturally belonging to the mother, since it was her body and she was the one most profoundly affected. I understood that, and yet it was turning out to be excruciating for me and my son to be pushed to the side, as if we didn't matter. Daniela's decision on this could force Justin into a fatherhood he wasn't ready for, but couldn't ignore.

As for me, I already loved this child, my grandchild, perhaps the only one I would ever have. Yet what say would I have in his life? How did I know that Daniela and her family wouldn't move off to Chile, never to return?

Justin's next words shocked me.

"Miss Kris, the sex ed teacher, says that getting pregnant in high school basically ruins your life."

My mouth fell open. The fact that this woman might be right was beside the point. How dare she put ideas like that into my son's head?

"Miss Kris needs to shut her mouth when she's clueless about something," I flared. "You listen to me, Justin. Your life will be different—and, yes, challenging—because of this. But it's all what you make of it. Just keep stepping up to the plate the way you have been. Life will sort itself out."

"Yeah, right."

"You never know how life's going to go, honey. Things that seem bad turn out okay sometimes."

A sad smile came to his face. "Okay, thanks, Mom." He took a long, slow look around.

"It'll be okay, love."

He nodded. "This room's all right, I guess."

I raised my eyebrows. "This room's *cool.*"

"Can I sleep out here tonight?"

I cast a dubious eye around me. "It's not very comfortable right now."

"I'll put a sleeping bag on the floor." He was already starting out the door to get it, but then he turned back. "Mom?"

"What, honey?"

"*You're* cool. Thanks."

"You're welcome."

It was my job, I told myself, to help my kid find strength during this hard time. To help him keep hope alive.

Chapter 20

When I got to the house, I stuck my head through the door of Caroline's screened porch. She lay curled on her side on the bed, her back to me.

I'd just made one person I loved feel better. Why not go for two? Maybe I would feel better in the process.

"Hey, sister of mine, may I come in?"

She looked over her shoulder at me, her face mottled and red from crying.

Wordlessly, I slipped onto the bed next to her and put my arms around her. I couldn't imagine what Caroline was going through. Grant was amazing—loyal and sensitive and one of the smartest guys I'd ever met. I'd never had a relationship that came close to theirs.

Spooning with my sister, I rubbed my forehead between her shoulder blades. "What can I do for you?"

"Just stay with me."

We lay there while I drifted in and out of a light sleep. Her warmth, the softness of the bed, the pure relaxation of it—Caroline and I had slept like this together when we were little, but since then, I'd never been much of a spooner.

"Nicole?" Caroline's voice cut a path through my thoughts. "Remember what Mom used to say? You know, when one of us was sad and needed a shoulder to cry on?"

"I remember."

We said the words together. *"Get over it!"*

Her shoulders shook as she laughed. "That was Mom. The proverbial soft place to fall."

"Yeah, like a bed of nails."

"I miss her."

"Me too."

Caroline looked over her shoulder at me. "What would I do without you, Nicki?"

"Starve and die? Be laid to rest in a lonely grave?"

"Probably. But still." She rolled over to face me. "As the older sister, I get to set you straight every once in a while."

"Set me straight? About what?" I said, astonished but encouraged by her sudden mood change.

She stared into my eyes, her own still red and puffy, her hair in a state of advanced bedhead. "About Mike."

"What about him?"

"He's totally in love with you. He has been for years."

I sat up. "Be serious."

"And you're in love with him. You're just too busy being Little Miss Independent to see it."

I jumped up from the bed, not sure how everything had changed in just a second.

"A relationship doesn't have to be like yours and Brady's," Caroline said. She had come up to sitting and was holding her head up bravely. "Even if I never speak to Grant again, I had his love for years, and that was real. And no one can ever take that time away from me." She grabbed a tissue and blew her nose.

"I'm so sorry all this happened to you."

"I'm not." She gave her hair a dramatic swoop. "I gave my heart and loved, and it was worth it. That's what you should do. Without that, you'll never have fully lived."

"Wow," I said slowly. "I'm not fully alive. Is that what you're saying?"

"I'm just saying that you have true love staring you right in the face, and—"

"Stop. Just stop, Caroline." A wave of weariness hit me. I

forced myself to count to ten before I spoke. "I can't do this right now, okay?"

I turned my back on her and left. Not fully alive, my ass.

I had a child; Caroline didn't.

I had a real career; Caroline didn't.

She'd been the one who'd found love with a wonderful man—but it was gone now, which only went to prove my point.

I was just as alive as she was, wasn't I? Maybe just in a different way.

But when true love is staring you right in the face . . .

I had a box for that idea. I did the only thing I could and stored it in a faraway dark corner of my mind.

Two evenings later, I was once again toiling at my potter's wheel, the wet clay cool and resistant under my fingers. This was one of those times when it would not be tamed, slithering out from under my hands, folding over on itself, or dissolving into nothing.

I was playing hooky, doing something that had nothing to do with making money or art. I had given up mass production for the day and was experimenting with an eggshell-thin bowl—too thin really for the clay to handle. I knew it was too thin, which was why it wasn't working, but pure ego drove me on. I was master of the clay, and blast it all, it would bend to my wishes!

The halfway finished pot collapsed in my hands, causing a spot of pain to begin building in the center of my forehead. Frustrated, I ripped the clay from the broken pot off the wheel and hurled it to the floor.

Everything sucked. My life was falling to pieces. My son was catatonic. My grandchild's future seemed ruined before it started. The due date for the mural, three weeks from now, was bearing down upon me with the speed and ferocity of an oncoming train. I hated the pottery I'd shipped last week: pieces without the subtle variations that made each item unique and just a little out of the ordinary. That mattered to me, even for commercial work, and I was losing it in this race for speed and quantity.

My eye fell on my labeled pots of glaze—Not Your Ordinary Blueberry, Not Your Ordinary Olive Green—fifteen shades in all. Knowing that my glazes were special, I had another ten colors planned, among them a luscious cantaloupe, a creamy pale yellow, and a purple so deep it verged on black. They were gorgeous and easy to use too, as they cleaned up easily and dried quickly. But even my glazes hadn't been enough to salvage this latest shipment of ho-hum pottery.

I should look at the bright side. It didn't matter that there would be no money for Justin's college because early fatherhood would prevent him from going, anyway. He'd be working as a bartender somewhere. Maybe he could get me a job at the same place, and we'd become a mother-son bartending duo. He and his child, another boy, would live with me forever, and I would effectively raise little Maximilian to become a third-generation bartender. Or perhaps a fine, upstanding young shoe salesman.

"What's wrong?" Daniela was cleaning brushes at my giant stainless steel sink.

"Nothing really, honey." Once again, I was determined to keep my adult problems to myself as much as I could. "I'm just thinking about how to make my pieces as good as possible. It's a little harder when I'm making more of them."

Daniela drew her eyebrows together as she tried to understand. "Why do you need to make more pieces?"

I tried to sound casual. "Just to make a little more money."

"Oh." Daniela's brow cleared. "Too bad you don't have a machine to sell. Like Dr. Azirian."

"Who?" Then I remembered. The obstetrician that Viviana had worked with. Doctors were well paid, but, like me, their pay was basically limited by the number of hours in a day. There were only so many patients that one could see in twenty-four hours. But this doctor had invented something she could manufacture and sell in large numbers. And she was raking it in.

An idea floated through my head but didn't quite take hold. It floated away.

"Nicole?" Daniela was looking thoughtful as she shook off a batch of brushes and laid them out to dry.

Something in the tone of her voice caught my attention. "Yes?"

"I don't want the kids at school to know about the baby. Not before summer break, anyway." She picked up a large brush coated in dry, hardened glaze and put it in water to soak.

"We only have a couple days of classes left, then a week of finals," she added. "Do you think I could get away with wearing these big T-shirts?"

I inspected her. She'd been enjoying eating for two, packing away the pasta and mashed potatoes, so she'd gained a few pounds. It only served to make her look curvy and pretty. "I think so. Just don't tell anyone. Not even Heather."

How come I hadn't thought about this earlier? It was obvious there would be giant repercussions for Justin and Daniela at school. Ordinarily, I would have paid more attention, but the hugeness of this crisis, combined with work obligations, seemed to have blown a fuse in my brain. Some of the lights were simply out.

She looked so relieved that I felt sorry for her. Pregnant, separated from her parents, unable to speak to friends.

"Look, I know we've just met, but for what it's worth, I'm here. If you need someone."

A real smile now. "Thanks. That means a lot."

Chapter 21

I was digging through a closet in my studio when I came across one of Justin's old basketballs. He and Mike had played a lot of one-on-one at the hoop we'd installed at the car park, but he'd also liked doing fancy dribbling or tricks, like twirling the ball on one finger or tossing it up and catching it behind his back.

On an impulse, I took the ball with me to the house at dinnertime. For a change of pace, we were going to eat inside, although we would keep the French doors open to bring in fresh air.

The main living area in my house was of the open-concept variety, where the kitchen occupied one wall across from an island of cabinets and countertop.

On the other side of the island sat my so-called living room, my undistinguished but comfortable sofa, armchair, and beanbag chair, all arranged to form a rough conversation circle with the four stools at the island. A once beautiful rug and ancient coffee table filled the center of the circle.

Finally, beyond the living room was a wide strip of open floor that ran between the back of the sofa and the wall of French doors opposite the kitchen. It was a traffic area that one walked along to reach the bedrooms or crossed to exit to the patio and backyard. Years ago, Justin had dubbed it the "runway," and the name had stuck.

Mike was coming to dinner tonight, as well as Jamie. They were such regulars to the house that I thought of this as family time. Both of them were in the kitchen when I arrived, hanging out at the island with Caroline and a pitcher of margaritas. Mike had his usual Corona.

I clicked my tongue in mock disapproval. "Start without me, why don't you?"

Mike walked over to me. "Sorry." He crushed me into another one of his bear hugs, while the basketball bounced away.

Breathless, I wiggled around in his arms. Caroline's words must have gotten to me, because I found myself noticing how good he smelled, how warm he was, how hard his arms and chest were.

"Look what I found!" Still immobilized in his arms, I nodded in the direction of the basketball.

"I saw." He released me and went after the ball, calling for Justin, who appeared in the runway from the bathroom.

"Check it out! We should play after dinner." Mike shot the ball across the room to Justin, who caught it.

Jamie kissed me hello. "Hey, Grandma," she whispered in my ear.

"I know, can you believe it?" I drew her into my bedroom and shut the door so we could talk for a minute. "This is so terrible for Justin. But if I think of myself, just for a second, and I picture a new baby to take care of . . . it's pretty exciting!"

"Better you than me." Jamie had never seen the point of babies. "More importantly, when are you going to put that adorable man out of his misery and sleep with him?"

"You too? What is this? You sound like Caroline."

"I've never sounded like Caroline in my life."

I had to laugh. There were no two people more different than she and my sister. "You know he has other women."

"Well, I would hope so. What else is he supposed to do when you hold out on him?"

"Jamie! He's my friend."

"Friend, schmend! He would jump your bones in a second if he knew you were open to it." Jamie raised her eyebrows at me. "You're just lucky he's still waiting around for you."

Even if I could have come up with a reply, she didn't give me the time. "Damn! I need another margarita." She drew me back out into the living room. From the outside, through the open doors, came the sound of my wind chimes on the night breeze.

Mike and Justin stood in the runway tossing the ball back and forth while Daniela watched, mouth open in astonishment. "You're allowed to play ball in the house?" she asked.

"It depends on what kinda mood Mom's in," Justin said.

"It's okay. Just be careful." I was thrilled to see him having fun, if only for a moment. The only things in the room I worried about were my big ceramic candlesticks, which stood on a low table in the corner. "I'll move these out of the way."

Jamie helped me take them into my bedroom. "Whoa, they're heavy!" she said.

"Tell me about it." I lifted them easily, though, strong from years of hefting tableware and other pottery. "They're safe now, anyway."

"The rest of our stuff, she'd thank me for breaking it," Justin said.

"I wouldn't go that far." Like old times, Justin had gotten me cheerful again. "Honey, show us some of your tricks."

"Nah, I'm rusty." But his hands continued to caress the ball. He flipped it around a few times and dribbled it underneath one leg, then the other.

Caroline had put a casserole pan and other serving dishes on the kitchen island. "Help yourselves!" One by one, we did, filling our plates and choosing among the motley seating options. Caroline, who didn't like eating from a plate in her lap, took a stool at the kitchen island, and Jamie joined her a minute later. Mike, as usual, took the armchair, while Daniela snuggled into the beanbag chair. Alone in the sofa, I sat sideways on it, my back against the arm, so I could easily see Justin in the runway by looking to my right.

Playing with the basketball, he balanced it on the tip of his index finger and set the ball spinning, then popped the ball up to land on the tip of his middle finger, and then onto his pinky, spinning continuously the whole time.

"Which finals do you still have to take?" I asked.

Justin blew out a deep breath, his face falling. "Calculus, History, and a paper for Honors English." He tossed the ball from his pinky into the air and caught it. "The paper's almost done."

"Are you ready for the tests?"

"I will be." His voice quavered as his eyes fell. These grades were the most important, the last ones seen by the colleges before they made their decisions.

I glanced over at Daniela, who sat quietly, listening intently. "How about you, Daniela?"

She shrugged. "Physics is freaking me out a little. The rest are okay."

Justin jumped and took another imaginary shot. "He scores!" Seeing Mike bent over his phone in the armchair, absorbed in a text, he said, "What about those hoops, dude?"

Mike's head snapped up. "What?"

"Hoops. We were going to play after dinner."

Mike's pleased expression vanished. "Oh, man, I forgot. I made other plans. Sorry."

"No worries, dude." Justin spun the ball and executed an imaginary dunk shot.

"Tomorrow, for sure." Mike finished his text and stood up.

I knew him too well; I knew the direction that his evening agenda had taken. I usually didn't give much thought to the women Mike had seen over the years—some married, some just friends with benefits—but today I felt a pang. Who was she, and what did she mean to him? One of these days, he might find one he really liked, and then where would I be?

As I walked him to the door, I wanted to say, *Stay awhile.* But I couldn't. Instead, I said, "Booty call?"

He paused for a moment, his face bland and expressionless. "You have a problem with that?"

"No! No, not at all. Go on now and . . . enjoy!"

Enjoy? How idiotic. I wanted to sink into a hole in the ground. And even worse, tears were now prickling the backs of my eyes. Mortified, I gasped out, "Bye," and wheeled around to leave.

"Hey!" He had taken my arm. "You okay?"

Furious with myself, I dabbed at my eyes. "Yeah. It's just . . . it's been rough lately. With Justin and the baby, you know."

"I know. Let's sit down for a minute."

We walked out to the picnic table.

He took on a light tone. "Course, you're not upset because . . . because I'm . . . ?"

"Not at all!"

"Because we're just friends, right? We're both free to date anyone we want."

"Oh, I do! I mean, I have!" Eight years ago, at least.

He was too much of a gentleman to comment. We sat on the bench together, peaceful, side by side, like two old people. He took my hand.

"Don't you have to go?" I said.

"In a minute." He showed no signs of moving.

In the cool night, his body radiated heat. I shivered a little, wishing I could lean up against him.

"You cold?" He put his arm around me and, bliss! I got to snuggle against his ribs.

"Mike?" I found myself asking, "How come you've never settled down? Don't you want to get married and have kids someday?"

He thought for a minute, then spoke, placing each word carefully. "I like my life," he said. "Travel, exciting work. Good friends."

"Women," I added.

"Yeah, I've known some pretty interesting women. But . . ."

"But what?" I asked, hoping for the perfect reply. *But none as beautiful and enchanting as you, Nicole.*

Crickets chirped. Centuries of silence rolled by.

"Have you ever been in love?" I asked, then immediately cringed. *Since me,* I added mentally. If he had ever loved me.

More silence. Then, "Yeah." That one word, then nothing.

My throat and eyes ached suddenly at the thought. In love with whom? Me? Caroline obviously thought so.

"So," I insisted, "what happened?"

"It's complicated." He cleared his throat suddenly and shifted his position, looking at me with curiosity. "Where's all this coming from? These questions?"

"I just . . ." I plucked up my courage. "Do you ever think about us, Mike? Back when we were . . ."

His eyebrows raised. "When we were . . . what?" He was ribbing me, but gently.

"Mike!"

He relented. "Yes. I think about us."

"Why did . . . ?"

He paused. "I guess our timing was off." His look seemed to mirror my feeling—a blend of surprise, irony, and resignation. "Or maybe," he added, "I wasn't ready back then." He seemed to remember he had somewhere to go and stood up.

I watched him leave, wondering what he meant by that last statement. *I wasn't ready back then.* If this man was ready now, if he loved me, what was he doing running into the arms of another woman? What would happen if I took him into my own arms? What if I opened my heart to him?

"Mom!" Justin was yelling for me.

When I returned to the living room, Caroline and Jamie were

doing dishes, while Daniela swept the floor. Justin, at long last, was filling his dinner plate.

"You're eating now?"

His eyes were remote again, his mind in some faraway place. "I'm gonna take this out to my room, okay?"

"Okay." My son would eat alone in his bedroom, and I, the bad mother, had allowed it to happen. Completely defeated, I let him go, just as I'd let Mike go a few minutes earlier.

Chapter 22

The next evening, I was up to my elbows in clay when Daniela called me on her cell. I frowned at the phone. Why was she calling me when she could just come into the studio? She knew it was hard for me to answer the phone when I was throwing pots.

My hands and nails heavy with clay, I stopped for a moment and listened. I'd programmed my phone to ring ten times before the voice mail picked up, something Daniela also knew. Her call went to voice mail.

A second later, it began to ring again. Concerned now, I moved to the sink and washed my hands and forearms as quickly as I could, while the second call went to voice mail as well. Drying myself with a towel, I found her message, stated in a thin, wavering voice. "Would you come down the road to get me, please? Right now? In your car?"

"On my way," I texted back.

Had she fallen? Broken an ankle? I grabbed my keys and ran.

Tonight, there was no moon. Damn the city for not lighting our road. I doubled back and grabbed a flashlight, wondering if Daniela had taken one, the way I kept telling her to.

As I rolled out of the car park, I cursed myself for not bringing Justin. What if she needed to be lifted or carried? I drove cautiously with my high beams on, fearing as I swung around each curve to find her right under my wheels.

There she was, waving her arms and running toward my car. She didn't seem hurt at all. "Daniela!" I called out the window. "Are you okay? What is it?"

She twisted the hem of her T-shirt. "Don't be mad. My mom,

well, she needs some help." She was pointing to a car parked in a pullout just in front of me. The blue Hyundai.

A sinking feeling came over me that my life was suddenly about to become very, very complicated. Feeling like I was moving through wet, heavy sand, I got out of the car.

"Please don't be mad," Daniela said again.

The woman sat very still in the front seat of the car, her arm at an odd angle in her lap. As she turned toward me, I saw the very faint dark hue of a bruise along one side of her face.

Daniela's mother spoke in her lilting accent. "I fell down the stairs." She grimaced. "I've got a broken arm."

"He was drunk again, wasn't he?" Daniela's eyes contained a sorrow as deep and wide as the ocean.

"It was an accident," Viviana told me.

"We've got to get this arm looked at." I pulled out my phone and hit the speed dial for home. "You and Caroline don't need to come," I told Justin. "But . . ." Suddenly, I thought of Mike's broad shoulders, his solid, reassuring presence. "Would you call Mike and tell him I'm taking Daniela's mom to Cedars Sinai hospital?"

At the emergency room, a nurse ushered in Daniela's mom, then handed me a clipboard. "Fill out these papers."

"Do you want me to fill this out for you?" I asked Daniela. "Or help you with it?"

"I think I can do it." We sat on the plastic chairs of the ER waiting room, Daniela hunched over the clipboard, gripping the pencil.

We were not alone. A woman and two boys sat to our left a few seats down. I assumed she'd had no one to leave the children with;

the little one lay asleep with his head in her lap. A trio of teenagers with multiple face piercings sat near the door and, by the admitting station, an old man mumbling under his breath to himself.

The scratch of Daniela's pencil caught my attention. I looked over her shoulder as she wrote. Patient name. *Viviana Harris.* Name of spouse. *Boyd Harris.*

These last few evenings, when Daniela had strolled off down the road, had she been meeting her mother? Daniela hadn't mentioned her mom, one way or the other.

"I don't know our insurance information," Daniela said in a defeated voice.

"Let's check your mother's purse."

Together, we went through it. With fumbling hands, I took out her wallet and opened it, pausing over a photograph of a man standing on what looked like a mountain hiking trail—a man with sun-burned red cheeks and a cheerful grin. The tousled dark-blond curls looked familiar. "Is that him?" I asked, unable to disguise the coldness of my voice.

She nodded, then snapped closed the photo section of the wallet, putting the picture out of sight.

"Honey, I'm so sorry you have to go through this." I tried to quell the uneasiness rising in me. I'd always thought that my disastrous marriage and divorce had toughened me up, made me into a strong person. Brady had always known the exact thing to say that would hurt me the most, that would slice right into the center of my being and cut me apart. But I'd never feared that he would break one of my bones, hit me, or knock me over.

What was Boyd capable of? Would he get inebriated, show up on our doorstep, and insist on taking Daniela? I had no right to keep her from him. I didn't know what he might do, and I didn't want to find out.

The ER was filling up. A huge guy in black leather pants, a

vest, and a motorcycle helmet limped in, his arms all scraped and bloody. A woman carried in a howling baby.

Catching a meaningful glance from the admitting nurse, I turned back to the forms. I found Viviana's insurance card, and together Daniela and I filled in the information. Relieved, I gave it to the admitting nurse, speaking to her for a few moments and returning to sit with Daniela, who perched on the edge of her chair, eager for news.

"What did they say?" she asked. "How's Mom doing?"

Again, my heart went out to this sweet girl with the sad, frightening life. "Fine. They've set her arm and will have her out to us in a minute." It was clear to me that Viviana had not told the doctors much, attributing her injuries to an accidental fall down the stairs.

"Has your mom ever had 'accidents' like this before?" I asked Daniela. "Something that sent her to the hospital?"

"No. Dad used to be a lot more low-key. And not only is Mom a nurse, but so's her cousin in Vegas. So when we lived there and Dad wasn't . . . as bad as he is now, she would treat herself or get her cousin to do it."

"What kinds of injuries?" I hadn't intended for my voice to sound so sharp.

Daniela evaded my question. "I'm so sorry for getting you involved."

I pushed away my doubts and spoke in the gentlest voice I could muster. "Instead of apologizing, why don't you tell me the whole story? And don't leave anything out."

"Everything was going okay," Daniela said. "At least," her voice faltered, "as far as I knew. But then something happened." She spoke apologetically. "He's okay most of the time. It's just when he drinks, he kind of changes personality. So, when we moved from Las Vegas out to LA, and I met Justin, and Dad found out . . . well, you know.

"And my dad was super mad at me, and Mom was worried." She stopped speaking again. "She'd heard me say that Justin's mom was really nice to his friends. So, she thought . . ." Daniela was speaking more and more slowly. "That maybe you would help me if I had no one else. Since my baby was your grandchild and all."

I tried to listen for what she wasn't saying. "So, in fact, it was your mom who decided . . . ?"

"Yeah. Mom wanted me in a safe place, especially after I got pregnant. She told Dad I ran away."

"Wouldn't he call the police?"

"He doesn't . . . really like to deal with the police."

Oh, really? I didn't find that comforting. "And your mother came to see you."

"She missed me, so she started coming up your road, she told me, just to catch sight of me. I didn't know until yesterday, when I spoke to her. I should have told you sooner." She trailed off miserably.

"It's okay."

I was about to pepper her with more questions when a flurry arose in the now crowded waiting room. Mike strode in like a man possessed. Straight from a movie set, he was in full cowboy gear—the boots, shirt, rodeo belt buckle, and jingling spurs. His eyes swept the room and landed on me.

I jumped to my feet. "Mike!"

In two steps, he was beside me. "Is everything okay?"

As I fell into his arms, I was dimly aware that applause had broken out. "I'm so glad to see you." I clung to him, relishing the feeling of comfort and safety he gave me.

His arms tightened around me for a long moment before he

released me. "Hey, squirt," he said to Daniela. Taking in her abject misery, he moved over to her and gave her a bear hug. She threw her arms around his neck.

After a second, he stepped away, his eyes moist, and dug into his pocket. "Damn, my wallet's back at the set with my regular clothes. I was gonna let Daniela go get herself some snacks."

I produced a five-dollar bill from my purse and handed it to Daniela. "Wanna go hit the vending machines?" I hated to see the apprehension in her eyes. She was still waiting for my response to her confession, but I needed to think and digest everything I'd heard.

"It'll be okay, honey," I managed to say. "We'll talk more later."

She smiled, her shoulders relaxing. "I'll bring you back something." She took off.

We sat down while people continued to stare at us.

"I have to get these things off." In two movements, he stripped off his spurs, then looked around, unsure of where to put them.

I reached out and took them from him, my hand dropping unexpectedly at their weight. They made an infernal jingling. Inspecting them, I saw the cause—there, rattling against their casings, were metal wheels with sharp points made to dig into the soft flanks of horses. Shuddering at the world we lived in, I dropped them into my cavernous canvas bag.

Seeing Viviana with her useless arm had shaken me. I'd never admitted to myself how important Mike was to me. What a delicious relief it was to have him here now, to have someone I trusted, someone who would drop everything to come to help me. A rock.

I was intensely aware of the fact that he had taken my hand. Our interlaced fingers felt oddly, almost inappropriately, intimate in this impersonal room full of strangers. He was speaking to me.

"Justin said it was Viviana who was hurt, but still, I got freaked out. I kept picturing you falling down the stairs, with a broken neck." His face was ashen.

"I'm fine." I told him everything, from Viviana's unexpected appearance to Daniela's story, while he listened and peppered me with questions.

"So Viviana specifically targeted you as someone who might take Daniela in?"

"Yeah, but it makes sense, right? I'm the baby's grandmother. Justin's the father. Of course she would turn to us."

"Okay, but why sneak around and make up stories? Why not just call you?"

"She must have had her reasons. I swear, Mike, in her shoes, I would have done it. To protect my kid? In a heartbeat."

Mike shook his head, as if he wasn't sure he bought it.

"I think she stayed with her husband on purpose. She figured, if she had Boyd's attention on her, he wouldn't think about Daniela."

"That's his name?"

I nodded.

Suddenly, Mike was looking past me. "There she is."

Viviana, calm and composed, stood next to an orderly. The only signs of injury were faint bruises on the side of her face and the plaster cast on her arm, which was in a sling.

She walked toward us, nodding her head to acknowledge Mike. "My, my, so many people at the hospital for me. And all because of a silly accident." Her eyes had gone remote, as if she'd fixed them inward on something inside her own head. She had a cool, impersonal aura about her that I hadn't picked up on before.

"All I did was lose my balance and fall down the stairs," Viviana said while Daniela stood silently by.

Mike nodded. I could see him turning the explanation over in his mind, evaluating whether he'd been justified in leaving Viviana in that house with her husband.

We gathered around Viviana. "We're releasing her," a nurse said.

Which raised the issue of where she would go. I saw my own

dismay reflected in Mike's eyes. Where *could* she go except my place? Apprehension coiled inside me as I thought of Mr. Boy Scout, of the pleasant smile and erratic temperament. *He doesn't know where Daniela's been staying,* I reassured myself.

Daniela was speaking to her mother in Spanish. *"Mama, no debes volver!"*

"Mija. I must go home," Viviana said.

"No!" The words burst from Daniela's lips.

I forced myself to speak. "Stay with us."

"It is better for Daniela if I go home," Viviana told Mike and me. "It is better for everyone."

I marveled at this woman who seemed utterly fearless when it came to protecting her child. "You shouldn't go back there."

Mike broke in. "Of course not. But she shouldn't go to your house, either."

What other choice was there at one in the morning? Besides, as much as I relied on Mike, it wasn't for him to say who could and couldn't stay at my house. I'd been making my own decisions for too long to start handing them over to him now. The imploring look from Daniela, the mingled hope and desperation in her eyes, pushed me over the edge.

"Don't worry, honey. Your mom's coming home with us."

Caroline and Justin had waited up for us. They watched as Viviana eased herself onto the living room sofa. Daniela perched beside her, looking frequently at her mother, as if for approval, her hands folded in her lap.

Justin stood next to me near the kitchen island, completely at a loss, shifting his weight from foot to foot, his hands dangling as if he didn't know what to do with them. Mike, on the other hand, was walking from window to window, inspecting. "You ever think of shutting these," he called to me over his shoulder, "and maybe locking them?"

I gave him a hard stare. "In the summertime? We'd roast."

Meanwhile, Caroline, in a bathrobe and fluffy slippers, had surged toward Viviana with offers of aspirin. "Or maybe some chicken soup? A little tapioca?"

Viviana produced a single word. "Whiskey?"

Caroline threw me a questioning look.

"We have whiskey," I said. "But is it a good idea with all the medication you've taken?"

"A little," Viviana pronounced, "is okay."

As a nurse, she ought to know.

I poured out a finger of whiskey and handed it to Viviana. "Mike?" I held up the bottle.

"No, thanks." He'd been examining the locks on the French doors, muttering to himself. He walked up to me and fastened a baleful eye upon me. "We need to put dead bolts on these doors," he said. We spoke in low voices so the others couldn't hear. "First thing tomorrow."

"I need to think about it." I'd supported and raised a child on my own. I didn't need a man to swoop in and tell me how to lock my doors.

"Nicole, what if this guy shows up here?" Mike asked.

"He doesn't know where Daniela's staying. Plus, it's not like he's some criminal. He's just a guy who drinks too much."

"I'm going outside. I want to look at your exterior lights." He disappeared before I could stop him.

I hoped Mike wasn't developing one of his fixations. When he got an idea into his head, he didn't stop until he'd carried it out to its fullest and furthest conclusion. He hadn't just taken a few flying lessons; he'd gotten a commercial pilot's license. He didn't just have a house built; he designed and constructed it with his own hands.

I didn't want him turning his prodigious energy and single-mindedness in my direction. He would erase me, reduce me to a pulp, and I couldn't go through that again.

And yet. I did have a few questions.

"Viviana," I asked, taking a seat at a stool at the island, "are you one hundred percent sure your husband doesn't know where Daniela's been staying?"

Her head pulled back ever so slightly, as if I'd offended her. "Yes, I am sure." She continued to sit on the sofa, with Daniela next to her. Caroline and Justin stood in the kitchen, listening.

I continued with my questions. "And how likely do you think he is to try to find you?"

"He already found us once," Daniela piped up.

"What do you mean?" I asked. "Was there another time he needed to find you?" At the same moment, Mike entered the room from the outside, stepping through the French doors.

Viviana placed her hand on Daniela's arm, giving her an icy look. "I am the mother! I will speak." She paused for a moment, as if gathering her thoughts. "Last June, Daniela and I moved to Los Angeles." She stopped.

"And . . . ?" I prompted.

Daniela burst in. "We ran away. We were hiding from him."

"We are very tired. Perhaps we can talk of this tomorrow," Viviana said quickly, casting a meaningful look at Daniela.

Caroline responded belatedly, as if hating to end the conversation. "You two must be exhausted."

I rose, my mind still racing with questions. "Yeah. We need to get you some other clothes and sort out the beds."

Not to be left out, Daniela tagged along with us into my bedroom, where I found her mom a soft, oversize T-shirt and a new toothbrush. Mike, I noticed, followed us discreetly.

"You are very kind," Viviana said.

"I'm happy to help. But would you mind if I asked a few more things?"

For a split second, Viviana made a face that I would have called annoyed. "It is late."

"Yes, but this is important." I was surprised that, after the way we'd gone out on a limb for her, she wasn't more gracious about it. But she was no doubt in pain, frightened, and exhausted. Caroline and Mike, I noticed, were waiting to hear what Viviana had to say.

"I'll be quick. Tell me about you and Daniela coming to Los Angeles."

Little by little, the story came out. In Las Vegas, Boyd had struck Daniela. It was in the face, just once, but he had never touched her before.

"I knew I had to take her away," Viviana said.

"Is that when you came to LA?" I asked.

Viviana hesitated. "Yes. Just Daniela and me. We ran away from Las Vegas and hid from him here."

Both a flutter and a pounding in my chest. "But he found you anyway?"

When Viviana didn't answer, Daniela broke in. "Yes. He made Mom's cousin give him our address and came to LA and rented a house. He came and . . . took us." She didn't try to disguise the anger and fear in her voice.

"Took you?" The hair raised on my arms. I glanced over and saw Caroline go white.

"He asked us to come with him to our new home," Viviana said.

"He said he would make us very sorry if we didn't come." Daniela had both fists clenched, her eyes blazing.

"To that pink house?" More fear began to thread its way

through my body. Boyd Harris had spared no energy or expense following his two women to Los Angeles and finding them. Caroline was gazing at me with huge, reproachful eyes that said, *How could you have gotten us into this?*

"Yes." Daniela went on. "He thinks it's funny to make us live there, because he knows we hate it. He calls it our payback for leaving him."

My stomach churned. Boyd Harris had found his wife and daughter once before when they went into hiding. What would stop him from doing it again?

What kind of man was he, anyway? Was he an otherwise upstanding citizen whose nasty habit was to knock around his weaker family members? Or was he dangerous to anyone who crossed his path?

Fear coiled inside me. And yet, the mere thought of this man raising a finger against Justin got my protective juices flowing. I believed those stories about mothers who lifted entire automobiles off their children's bodies. Mere tonnage couldn't stop a mother who was hell-bent on saving her child.

If some bad guy even looked twice at my son, I would protect him like a mama mountain lion with a migraine. And PMS. Nothing was going to happen to Justin.

I would enlist Jamie's help. She'd been a paralegal for a criminal defense firm and could track down anything I needed to know about Boyd Harris. I'd give her a shout tomorrow.

Caroline was preparing to dig in her heels. "They can stay here tonight, but we need a better solution long-term."

"We'll talk more later." I wasn't going to have this conversation in front of Viviana and Daniela. "Bedtime!" I said, turning drill sergeant. "Kids, you've got school tomorrow. Everyone, please, five minutes apiece in the bathroom—except for you, Viviana, of course."

"Mom can have my bed," Daniela said. "I'll take the sofa."

"Thank you, but she'll take my bed so you can both get a good night's sleep."

"What about you getting a good night's sleep, Mom?" Justin said.

"Don't worry about me. I'll be fine." I would be up for a while, and so, I suspected, would Mike and Caroline.

Chapter 23

We couldn't talk inside. Daniela and Viviana would have heard us through the walls. The three of us picked our way across the grass in the darkness and held our conversation out on the edge of the lawn, overlooking the lights of the city.

"I don't want them here!" Caroline's eyes had shrunk down to little slits, and her jaw had taken on that look of mule-like stubbornness that I'd seen on just a few occasions. Like when she'd decided to marry Grant. "That man's going to come for them. He's got a history of it!" As a cool night breeze blew, the three of us huddled together for warmth.

"He doesn't know where they are."

"He will, though," she said. "They have to get out of here tomorrow."

"You're forgetting that if he hurts Daniela, he could hurt the baby. That baby's ours just as much as it is theirs."

She gave me an anguished look. "It's putting us in danger."

"The real problem is Viviana. You heard her. If Daniela's here alone, he may leave us be."

"Then Viviana can go. Tomorrow. We'll give her a few nights in a hotel and then . . . *sayonara!*" Caroline wiggled her fingers to say goodbye.

We couldn't afford to give her a few nights in a hotel. I thought of my checking account and PayPal balances, all down to about a few hundred dollars.

Mike began to pace back and forth across the grass. "I agree that they can't stay for long, but we can install security. That'll help."

An automatic protest rose up inside me. *This is my home, not yours.* Besides, I already saw the place he was going, and it was expensive. "What kind of security? I have no money for an alarm system!"

"We'll work it out," Mike said. "I'll stay here tonight. Tomorrow, we'll see what we can do."

I was too tired to argue. We went back to the house, where I made up the sofa for myself with unsteady fingers, then tried to decide where to put an air mattress for Mike.

No spot was just right.

The most quiet, private place was on the floor next to the sofa where I was sleeping, but it seemed like putting our beds three inches apart might send a message I didn't intend.

The kitchen was likely to get traffic during the night, and the area by the French doors seemed wide open and vulnerable.

I put him by the French doors.

Mike took one look at my arrangement. "Hell no."

He dragged the air mattress over to lie beside me and the sofa. "For security purposes only," he cracked, heading back to the broken window latch he'd been repairing. "Don't get any ideas."

I put a fluffy down mattress pad on top of the air mattress, along with fresh cotton sheets and good pillows. He'll be comfortable here, I thought, patting the improvised bed.

When he returned, I was already tucked into my spot on the sofa.

"I'm gonna keep an eye out," he said. "For a while, anyway." He sat down on the bed I'd made for him, his back against the sofa. One part of me suddenly longed to snuggle my face up close to the back of his neck. I wouldn't let myself.

"We gonna be okay, Mike?" Even as I spoke, sleep tugged at me.

He looked back at me over his shoulder, his gaze reassuring. "You bet. We'll deal with it."

"I won't let you pay for a security system," I mumbled into my pillow, my eyes closing against my will.

"It won't cost much. You'll see."

I was able to get out two more words. "You promise?"

I fell asleep before I heard his answer.

The next morning, we were up and running, despite the long, tiring night we'd had. Only Viviana stayed in bed. Mike left early in search of locks and—who knew what else? Pots of boiling oil to pour from the roof, maybe. The kids went off to take the last of their final exams, for which they couldn't possibly be prepared. I hadn't seen either of them crack a book in two days, and it hadn't occurred to me to care. I was falling apart as a mother at the time when I most needed to be strong.

I had to pull it together, be productive. I put in a call to Jamie at the television studio.

"This is Jamie. Talk to me."

From the whoops and guffaws drifting out of the speakerphone, I guessed that a writers' meeting was in progress. "Do you know how to do a background check?"

"Does an egg roll? Does butter fly?"

"What?"

"That means yes. You want me to check out the A-hole? The one Viviana married?"

"That would be Boyd Harris, yes."

"Done. I gotta go. I'm workin' here!" More laughter from the speakerphone.

"Thanks." I clicked off and went to find Caroline. She and I were trying to go about our normal activities, but she was too scared to go out and weed the garden. As far as she was concerned, an angry and violent man could show up in our yard at any moment.

"He doesn't know where Daniela is," I said for the tenth time.

"How can you be so sure? He could have found out by now."

"We can't let this guy run our lives. I'll go with you to the garden. We'll take our pepper spray with us." We positioned ourselves to face the side gate where one entered the yard. The minute we saw him, we would sprint for the house or blast him with our spray cans.

I wasn't usually the fearful type. The warm sunshine and pleasant breeze made it hard for me to believe that an evil presence was stalking us out there.

Caroline, on the other hand, was falling apart. Every noise from the bushes, every rustle of a leaf or snap of a twig made her jump and look around. When a squirrel leaped onto a branch, rocking it up and down, she dug her fingernails into my arm so hard that I yelped. And when a man entered our yard, she screamed as if she were being disemboweled. "It's him! He's here!"

Clumsy me. In grabbing for the pepper spray, my hand accidentally knocked it into the petunias. I had snatched up a garden trowel and leaped to my feet, ready to gouge out an eye or two, when I realized it was Stefan, along with a bunch of workmen in tow.

Mike had called him. I just knew it. Mike had met Stefan through me years ago and was now his friend, as well as stunt coordinator on many of his films. As such, he'd become an expert on horror stunts and could tell you exactly how to kill a vampire with a stake or crush a bunch of zombies under the rubble of a falling building.

It was sweet of him to call Stefan. He just wanted to protect me. Why did that make me so uncomfortable?

Wolfgang ambled over, drooling, his jowls flapping. Happily, he plowed into the center of my flower bed to say hello. A couple of blooms detached themselves and stuck to his floppy ears, making him look like a girl with flowers in her hair. I scratched his silky head.

Stefan had brought with him Diego, his set construction supervisor, whom I'd known forever, as well as the workmen. Spontaneous, flamboyant, and insanely generous with his friends, Stefan had sent his workers my way occasionally over the years when they were in between films and I needed new bookshelves or cabinets. But those were small acts of generosity, where I could find a way to reciprocate.

Stefan waved to me as he walked around the yard with Diego, gesturing and pointing and discussing the work to be done. I struggled with a mixture of sweet relief and outrage. I was so lucky that I was not alone, that I had wonderful friends willing to step up and help me. And yet, how dare they presume to install things on my property without my permission?

"That traitor!" I hissed to Caroline. "Mike swore he wouldn't turn this into a big deal, and now he's brought in Stefan's crew. I can't afford to do this."

She pursed her lips and glared at me. "Who cares?"

"What . . . ?"

Caroline grabbed me by the shoulders. "Nicole! Now is not the time for denial." She spoke slowly, emphasizing each word. "This is a dangerous situation. Don't pretend it isn't."

Stefan and his guys were heading in our direction. I glanced over at them.

Caroline shook me to get back my attention. "For once in your life, let your guard down. Let him help us. I want this, and I own half this house. Do it for me. And for Justin."

Numbly, I nodded as the guys walked up to us. I would accept the help and pay them back. How many hundreds of dollars an hour did they cost?

"Mike called me," Stefan said.

Hah! I knew it!

"He says you need a few security measures." Whatever else he might have wanted to say was drowned out by the roar of a truck making its way up the Trail of Terror. The crew took off in the direction of the car park to meet it.

"Stefan, what do you know about home security?" I was too rattled to be diplomatic.

He waved a hand in the air. "Why, everything, darling. What is security, after all, but lights and cameras?"

"Explain to me what you're doing."

"It's very simple. We're going to install motion-sensitive lights and cameras. It shouldn't take more than half a day."

"How many? How much do they cost?"

"At least ten, if you consider the yard, the car park, and three-quarters of a mile of road."

I saw my IRA being gutted and cast aside, empty. "I can't afford to pay for this."

"Please. Do not insult our friendship." He fired off instructions at Diego, leaving him in charge, then said goodbye to me, European-style, with a kiss to each cheek.

As the workers did their jobs, I called Mike and ranted at his voice mail. For probably the first time ever, he failed to return my call, indicating just how determined he was to do this.

Four hours later, the work was done. If someone dared to come near us after dark, my property would light up like Disneyland, while prominently placed cameras would document the intruder's progress.

"They'll see us from outer space!" Justin said when he and Daniela got home from school. He had found Caroline and me in the kitchen, while Daniela had gone directly to my bedroom to see her mother. Viviana had spent the day in bed, sleeping and recovering. Low voices speaking Spanish came through the wall.

Justin scavenged through the pantry shelves for snacks, emerging with a bag of dried apple slices. "So Mike did all this for us? Where is he?"

"Mike and Stefan did it. And Mike's probably hiding from me," I said grimly, although I had to admit how grateful I was to have lights, finally, on our road and outside the house. I knew Stefan made something like twenty million dollars a year; the cost of this was pocket change to him. Mike made good money too, nothing like Stefan, but still. He could afford things. He had obviously worked out some kind of deal with Stefan to repay him or share the cost.

Why did I hate so much to feel that I owed either of them? Neither Stefan nor Mike would accept repayment in money, so I'd have to figure out some other way. Like a lifetime supply of free ceramics. Or coupons for a thousand homemade dinners under my twinkle lights.

Even as I sent up a prayer that Mike was done with his home improvements, we heard the rumbling of a motor, this one even louder than Stefan's truck from this morning. "I'll scope it out," Justin said. He returned a few seconds later, saying, "You guys have to see this."

As Daniela and Viviana were still holed up in my bedroom, the three of us—Justin, Caroline, and I—dashed out to the car park. There we saw a bulky vehicle grinding its way up the narrow Trail of Terror, tearing leaves and snapping branches as it went.

After a minute, it entered the car park, a grinning Mike at the wheel. He pulled up beside us. "Top of the line! Anyone want a tour?"

"Is that a mobile home?" I stood next to the driver's window, peering in at him.

He looked like a little boy who'd just gotten a new catcher's mitt for Christmas. "I borrowed it from a friend. I went to Palm Springs to get it."

I didn't know if I wanted to kiss this crazy, wonderful man or kill him. "Why? You going on a road trip?"

"I'm going to live in it."

"Where?" I already knew.

"Here. In the car park." His tone permitted no argument. "You promised I could install security."

Security as only Mike could provide it, and there was nothing I could do about it.

"This thing's a beast!" Justin said, and I knew immediately that a new name had been coined.

As if to cement that idea into place, Justin opened the door of the Beast, causing the dogs to spill out. It took mere seconds for Midge and Margo to mark every corner of the car park with their pee, barking to the world, *This is our territory now.*

Chapter 24

Later in the day, during that quiet hour before dinner, I took Mike aside. "Do you want to take a walk?"

"Do you want to see my new digs?"

"Sure." I gave him a sideways look. The laugh lines around his eyes looked especially deep today, as he'd been awake most of the night listening for prowlers. He reached out and put his arm around my shoulders. I didn't shake it off. I couldn't remember anymore why I didn't want him. Caroline had said he was my true love, and she knew me better than anyone.

How would it feel to let someone special into my life, someone I liked and trusted? Mike wasn't Brady. He was a real friend. And he smelled like peppermint.

I slid my arm around his waist.

We walked through the yard and out the side gate to the car park where the Beast stood. Mike opened the door and followed me up the two metal steps into his new abode. I stopped by the driver's seat to view the minuscule living space before me, a vision in plastic and aqua that encroached upon me from every direction. The center aisle was so narrow that Mike and I couldn't stand in it side by side. I felt Mike's presence as he came up behind me, just an inch away.

I turned around to face him. "I have to talk to you. This is important." In the small space, he was so close that my chest brushed his, but before he could react, I jumped back from him.

He gave me a dry look. "If you do that again, I may have to throw you down and ravish you. Just saying." His tone and expression were light, but underneath, he wasn't kidding. At the prospect, a delicious shiver started at my female center and began working its way up, rendering me mute.

It was he who finally broke the silence. "What did you want to say to me?"

"Oh. Yes." I struggled to pull myself together, while he waited, amused. "First off," I said, "thank you. For the lights and all."

His face registered surprise and then pleasure.

"It was generous and wonderful of you to do all this. We needed the help—I needed it." It was hard to get the words out. I tried to swallow past the lump in my throat. "So thank you."

"You're welcome." His eyes blazed with such warmth and love that it was hard for me to continue.

"I have something else to say. It's going to sound weird, but it's important to me," I said.

"Okay."

"Don't do it again. Not like that, anyway."

A flash of . . . something. Not anger, but maybe impatience. Or caution. "What do you mean?"

"I mean that if you and I disagree on something that concerns us both, I'd like to talk about it and work out our differences. I don't want you to just go off and do whatever you feel like. Today, you get a pass, because Caroline wanted it and it was an emergency. But ninety-nine percent of the time, it's not okay. You can't just override me, as if my opinion's meaningless. Do you see what I'm saying?"

His eyes widened. A long pause, then in a grumpy voice, "Yeah, I guess. It's just . . . if some guy ever knocked you down a flight of stairs, I think I'd beat the shit out of him."

"Don't do that. I don't want you arrested." I was smiling at him, and he smiled back. He was just inches away.

"Me neither. I'll try not to bulldoze you." He gave me a mock scowl. "So long as you keep your windows locked."

Behind Mike, the door flew open.

"Dinner's ready." Justin stood there, misery etched across his face.

I noticed, as if seeing him for the first time in weeks, that his hair had grown down into his eyes and over his ears. When had that happened? It seemed so recently that he'd had it cut short. His hair growing back—it was funny how those normal, natural things continued to happen even when your life was being upended and nothing about it would ever be the same again.

"Your hair's in your face," I said, then wondered what difference it made when the world was crashing down around us.

He rummaged through his pocket, pulled out a wide terry cloth headband, and put it on, girl-style, using it to push his hair back off his forehead and behind his ears. I'd been made to understand this was a guy fashion among Generation Z these days.

Confronted by this new look, Mike stopped short. "What's that?"

In a toneless voice. "It's called the Man Band."

Mike took in the information, as well as Justin's obvious distress. "Got it. Okay. I'll see you guys inside." Mike clapped him on the shoulder as he left Justin and me alone.

"What's wrong?" I asked.

My son's eyes, now revealed, held a despair that hit me like a jolt of electricity. "It's all my fault," he said. "Everything's going to shit, and it's my fault."

"That's not true." I lied to him with all my heart, just wanting to erase the despair from his face.

"Who're we kidding, Mom? I probably flunked two finals today. Next year, there'll be a baby here."

"Honey, we'll work it out. You'll see. You'll go to college and have a career, and . . ." I paused, knowing I was flailing. "You'll learn the joys of being a father, sooner than you wanted, perhaps, but . . ." I stopped again. "Being a parent is a wonderful thing." My voice trailed off.

Justin groaned, and I had to sympathize with him.

"And, Justin, I'll help you take care of it, if necessary. I'd love to do that. I'd love to have another baby in my life."

"Well, that makes one of us." Justin's expression was transitioning from dull misery to acute suffering.

"I miss my friends," he said. "They know something's wrong, but I can't tell them anything, because we're keeping it a secret. I can't have 'em over to the house 'cause Daniela's here."

"It'll be different now that school's ended."

Justin sighed the deep sigh of a person under an endless curse. "May I eat dinner in my room? I don't want to sit in there with everyone."

I hated to say no, but I had to maintain some sort of structure in our lives, even now. "I'd prefer you to eat with us," I said as gently as I could. "It's a good habit, and we like your company."

He groaned but didn't protest. His shoulders slumped as we walked to the house for dinner.

Chapter 25

Once again, we ate indoors. As much as I hated to admit it to myself, the fact was that out there somewhere lurked Boyd Harris, who'd come home last night to find that his wife and kid had left him once again.

By now, he'd had twenty-four hours to drink himself into a rage. As darkness approached, I pictured him festering in his anger and putting away tequila shots. He would make calls to ask if anyone had seen them, then hang up, drink a bottle of vodka, and express his feelings by smashing dishes and framed photos.

Would he find out where they were? Would he come for them? Caroline was right that we would be much safer if Viviana left, but I couldn't stand the thought of handing her over to that man.

Caroline had also been right to insist that I accept all those locks and lights and cameras. They would help us now.

There would be no fresh air in the living room tonight. I checked both the back door and the French doors, but Mike had already made sure they were locked with brand-new dead bolts. The windows were locked but had no curtains. Before the new exterior lights, anyone could have stood outside, unseen, and watched us, while we saw only our reflected selves in the dark glass. Now, however, no one could approach without setting off a succession of bright exterior lights that stayed on for half an hour. We would test how well they worked tonight.

Caroline had come to me earlier, frowning. "I have to go grocery shopping for dinner, and my credit card's maxed out. Do you have any cash?"

"No." I was expecting some payments, but my merchants were taking their time. "Don't we have something you can serve?"

"I'll fake it." Sure enough, she pieced together a buffet of odds and ends: cherry tomatoes in a vinaigrette, pasta with pesto made from fresh basil from our garden, some leftover take-out pad thai, and mini pizzas from the freezer. I wouldn't have given the strange assortment a second thought had it not been for our cool, intimidating guest.

Daniela had brought two plates of food, one for herself and one for Viviana. We'd given her and her mother the best seats in the house, on the sofa. It actually held three, but by unspoken consensus, no one had asked them to scoot over. We all gave Viviana a wide berth.

"What's this?" the woman asked, staring down at her plate.

"Your dinner," Daniela replied. "Pizza, pad thai, and pasta with pesto." She giggled a little at the proliferation of Ps.

"How puhfectly peculiah!" Justin intoned, scrunching his brow and pulling his lip up, while Daniela giggled again.

Caroline walked over to give her nephew a mock smack. "Put a plug in it, punk!" she snapped, gangster-style, from the side of her mouth. Her eyes twinkling, she glanced over at Viviana.

I found myself doing the same.

Viviana wasn't smiling.

I'd never seen her before in anything close to a normal setting; even with her arm in a sling, she had magnificent posture and sat on our crumbling sofa like a queen surveying her subjects. She had that same weird aura as yesterday—icy and impersonal—not what I would have expected given the way we'd helped her. And Daniela.

She was surveying the meal set before her on a TV table with her lip curled. Next to her, Daniela sat utterly still, watching and listening. Usually chatty, she hadn't said a word to anyone except her mother since we'd convened for dinner.

Caroline and I took two stools at the kitchen island, while Mike sat as always in the armchair. Outside, the sky had darkened.

No one ate much, and, except for Mike, we all jumped like nervous cats when the air-conditioning came on.

Justin sat cross-legged on the rug, picking at his dinner plate on the coffee table. I stared at him for a moment. He looked awful, his eyes dull and his bare feet coal black on the bottoms. A large stain adorned the leg of his pants.

Then there was the Man Band. It must have been designed for boys with long hair that would flow back from the band and down to the shoulders. By contrast, Justin's shorter hair stuck up in little points. Uneasy, I found myself glancing over at Viviana for her reaction.

Trying to spear a cherry tomato with his fork, Justin sent it flying off the plate. It bounced onto the floor and rolled under the coffee table.

"Shit!" He dived after it, sliding under the table on his stomach and capturing the tomato, then bumping his head hard on the table as he came back up. "Fuck!"

"Justin!" I cried, mortified.

Viviana's face had turned even more sour, if that was possible. He was, after all, the boy who'd gotten her daughter pregnant, and now, in his first prolonged encounter with Viviana, was throwing food around and swearing like a sailor. Not to mention looking like he'd crawled out of a dumpster.

Justin knew better; he usually bathed and combed his hair. He was a polite kid. Everyone said so, I assured myself.

"Your language!" I told my son.

Sullen. "You said there was no such thing as a bad word."

"I also said that, since many people don't like hearing so-called swear words, it's considerate to refrain from using them." I turned to Viviana. "I'm sorry. I think we're all a little on edge tonight." As I said it, I felt a pang of disloyalty to Justin for allowing myself to feel embarrassed by him.

"Perhaps this is why the American children have problems with the drugs and the alcohol," she observed, almost as if she were talking to herself. "There are no rules for them. They do not groom themselves. They sit on the floor to eat."

Aware that Daniela was listening, I controlled my response. "We're informal in my family. It's how we are; it suits us."

She continued her musings. "Still. One must observe standards."

"Mom," Daniela ventured, her face scarlet, "Nicole's been so nice to us." As Viviana placed a firm hand on her sleeve, she stopped mid-sentence.

Viviana looked around her as if to acknowledge that she and Daniela were not alone in the room. No trace of apology about her. "I say only what I think." She curtly inclined her head toward me. "You have been very kind. You have my thanks for that."

I remained outwardly serene, but inwardly, I fumed. The Viviana I'd admired for protecting her daughter was turning into someone I didn't feel like having in my crowded home. For Daniela's sake, I held my tongue.

Daniela had flushed a deep red and glowered at her mother. After a minute, she got up, taking her plate to the kitchen.

"Daniela, come back here and finish eating!"

The girl ignored her mother, scraping the contents of her half-full plate into the garbage. Her face a thundercloud, she lingered for a while, tidying up.

Mike brought his plate into the kitchen.

Daniela fastened her attention upon him. "Do you know the Charleston? I'll teach you."

Mike was already shaking his head. "I don't think so."

"No, really. It's easy!"

In twenty years, I'd never seen him go near a dance floor. Now, he was looking at Daniela with amusement. But at the same time, I could see it. The wall was going up.

"C'mon, Mike, give it a shot!" Justin called out.

"Go, Mike!" Caroline yelled.

"It's simple, see?" Daniela demonstrated on the uneven kitchen floor tiles. "Back, forward, forward, back."

Mike watched her politely but didn't try it himself. The way his feet were planted, it would have been easier to move an Egyptian pyramid.

"Then you pick up speed. See? Back, *kick* forward."

"No." Mike crossed his arms over his chest as we all yelled encouragement.

"And *kick* forward." Her curls bounced and her eyes shone, while Mike's face reflected granite-like resistance.

"Dear God," Justin said, "someone give that man a board to break."

Daniela doubled over with laughter, the rest of us following suit.

"Daniela!" Viviana silenced us instantly. "Come sit here beside me!"

She turned her back on her mother.

"Now!"

Stricken, the girl meekly seated herself, while the rest of us, silenced, looked away. Darkness had fallen and our windows had once again become creepy, dark mirrors.

My ringtone. It was Jamie, calling with the results of her background check. I snatched up my phone and slipped into the bathroom. "What did you find out?"

Jamie didn't waste time. "This guy has a record, Nicole. Disorderly conduct, assault, sexual assault."

The outside lights flashed on, illuminating the yard and pool. Noises from the living room.

"Thanks, hon. I gotta go!" I raced down the hall, then stopped to peer around the corner into the living room.

Mike stood by the French doors with the dogs, who hurled themselves, barking, toward the glass. Viviana and Daniela had vanished into my bedroom, where they couldn't be seen from the patio.

I marched over to stand with Mike wearing my deliberately calm mother's façade, but inside thanking every angel in heaven that Mike was there. *Disorderly conduct. Assault. Sexual assault.*

"I don't see anything," Mike said. He opened the door and stepped out, while Caroline emitted a terrified little squeak. Justin had picked up his baseball bat and stood with it in both hands, as if waiting for a pitch.

Mike came back in. "Coyote."

The whole room seemed to let out its breath at once. "Forget the Beast," I announced. "Mike, would you and the dogs stay in the house with us tonight? You too, Justin."

Mike was studying me with a half-surprised expression.

"Do you mind staying in here? I'd feel safer having you close."

"No. I don't mind." A little smile slipped across his face.

I wouldn't tell anyone about Boyd's criminal past. It wouldn't help them to know, I rationalized. I tried to ignore a feeling of simple embarrassment. I'd been so foolish getting my loved ones into this huge mess.

That night when I crawled onto the sofa, Mike was on the floor beside me, only a few inches away. Justin was camped with the dogs on the other side of the island.

Mike reached up and took my hand and we lay there for a moment, knowing Justin could hear us if we spoke too loudly.

"How about that Viviana?" he said in a low voice.

"Yeah, can you believe she's the best parent Daniela's got? It's scary."

"True."

"We'd be safer if I made her leave tomorrow. But where can she go except back to Boyd? I feel crummy doing that to her."

"I'm not working for the next three days, so I can be here full time."

"Really? And the kids are out of school." We'd be safe with Mike here.

That meant, for the next three days, we could sit tight in our fortress at the top of the hill, lock ourselves away from Boyd, and figure out what to do next. I would gather around me the people I most loved, and at least one I didn't love so much, and we would stay safe and see this thing play itself out.

Chapter 26

The next day was unseasonably hot for May. Mike had pulled the Beast across the opening to the car park, so no outsiders could enter the property. I reminded myself that Boyd hadn't found us—couldn't find us—and that I had to put on a brave front for the others.

The property was closed to visitors and Mike was here. We would be fine.

Only the grouchy Viviana stayed in the house. The rest of them headed for the pool, while I trudged off to work in my studio, otherwise known as the inferno. Sweat trickled down my neck and between my breasts as I sat at the potter's wheel longing for cool, blue pool water. But no. A studio executive's wife wanted a half dozen serving platters decorated with superhero themes for use at her twin sons' sixth birthday party. Surely a pressing need like that had to be accommodated.

After finishing the sixth platter, I decided I'd earned the right to cool off. Ignoring that panicky feeling about my mural, which I still hadn't started, I jumped into the pool and joined the others in splashing each other and hitting a beach ball around. Half the time it went out, allowing me to enjoy the sight of Mike in swim trunks, dripping wet, leaping from the pool to retrieve it.

He had smooth, tan skin and muscles earned from a lifetime of hard physical work, hours of martial arts practice, and running with the dogs. He was beautiful, the sun was shining, and he was here to take care of us. The mere thought helped me relax.

After a while, Mike and I put two chaise lounges side by side in a spot of shade a ways off from the pool. I'd worn my navy one-piece with the white polka dots. It was decidedly not cool by young people's standards, but it had a kind of cute vintage quality and made me look shapely. I saw Mike sliding a quick glance down my body, subtly, so no one would notice. Except I did. "Eyes up here," I whispered, using two fingers to point to my own eyes.

Caught, he showed no remorse. "You can't expect me not to look when you're wearing that. I'm defenseless."

What were the rules in a situation like this? If I started a romance with Mike, would he expect to keep his other women? I couldn't live with that. Would we fall in love or lose our friendship?

I looked around at the others. Caroline, who'd just gotten a call on her cell, was walking into the house to talk in private. Justin swam laps while Daniela stood in the shallow end, her large T-shirt floating around her. Catching my eye, she climbed out, dragged a lawn chair over to us, and sat down next to me.

"Hey, sweetie," I said. "How you feeling?"

"I can't wear a bathing suit anymore. I'm too fat," she moaned, pulling at her T-shirt. She didn't look fat to me, but that just meant the big shirt was doing its job. The school year had ended with her secret intact.

I felt a surge of fondness toward her.

"I memorized where every single thing in the kitchen is," she had said to me the other day. "Just try me."

"Tea strainer."

She produced it from a drawer.

"Rice cooker."

She pointed to an overhead cabinet and swaggered. "Put me against anyone in kitchen cleanup, and I'll kick their butt!"

Now, settling into her lawn chair, she pulled her knitting out of her bag. She had taught Caroline how to knit and was threatening to do me next. "You're an artist! How can you not know how to knit?"

Was I an artist? I wasn't so sure anymore. Artists had ideas. They found inspiration in the people and events around them. The words how we live ran through my mind like a continuous feed, but they didn't trigger anything. I didn't know anything anymore. I didn't know who my son was, who I was, who to trust.

Daniela was still talking. She tsked her tongue at me. "What if you should have a sudden need for a cable knit sweater? If you knew how to knit, you could just whip one up!"

"Who needs cable knit sweaters in Los Angeles? Can you knit me a bikini?"

"Yeah," Mike said. "Can you knit her a bikini?"

Daniela put on a playful, supercilious look. "I will *teach* you how to knit a bikini."

"Daniela!" The sharp voice tore through the air.

Instantly, the sparkle dimmed in Daniela's eye. Her smile dropped away. "Mom?"

"Don't you understand that you're bothering these grown-ups." Viviana had emerged from her lair. She'd managed to put the hand from her unbroken arm on her hip. She stood a few feet away in the grass.

"She's no bother at all."

Viviana didn't even look my way. "Come! Find something else to do." To my distress, she hauled Daniela off.

I began to think about serving lunch. Mike still sat next to me in the shade, making notes in the margins of a script. I left him to explore the refrigerator and see what I could feed the troops. As I passed by Caroline's open door, I saw her seated on the bed in the darkness, her curtains still drawn. She'd been on the phone in her room most of the morning.

I stuck my head in. "You okay?"

Caroline sat straight-backed on the bed with her hands folded in her lap, her face composed. "That was Grant. He wants to see me."

"Really? Why?" Alarmed, I sat down beside her.

Caroline placed her words carefully, one or two at a time. "He says he made a mistake. He wants me back."

I put my hand on hers but didn't say anything. What would I know about a twenty-four-year relationship full of mutual love and intimacy? This was not in my repertoire of life experiences.

She continued to lay out careful little groups of words. "He says he still loves me. He never stopped loving me."

"So what's changed now?"

"He got a great job. From his friends with that startup in Venice? It's doing really well, and the job's perfect for him."

"That's it?" I couldn't believe it. "What happens if this new job goes under too? Will he leave you again?"

She shook her head. "I don't know. I don't know anything anymore."

"What're you going to do?"

"Talk to him. He wants us to go to his family's beach house for a few days and talk the whole thing through." She twisted her hands together. "I hate to leave you now, though. With everything that's going on."

"Go." I said it instantly. "Get out of this place and go put your marriage back together. Or whatever it is you wanna do."

Caroline started to cry. "I prayed for this. I dreamed he would call and beg me to come back, and now he has, and I don't know how I feel. I don't know if I can trust him the way I did before."

"So take your time. You don't have to decide anything right away."

"I still love him. And he says he loves me."

"Then go to the man. But he's got some big explaining to do."

"Yes, he does." She gave me a firm nod of the chin, then let her expression crumple. "I hate to leave you in the middle of this crisis. You need help and support."

"I've got Viviana for that."

Caroline whooped.

It was my turn to put my hands on her shoulders. "I'll be fine. You have something important to do now, so whether it's with Grant or without him, go take your life back."

That evening, Mike pulled the Beast aside so that Caroline could head down the Trail of Terror. I put on a smile and waved. In her own way, she'd been a rock too, during this crisis, keeping us supplied with food and putting a good dinner on the table every evening. I already missed my sister so much that my throat hurt. Feeling so worried for her, so protective, and yet hopeful, and above all, proud. What a good, sweet, awesome big sister I had.

Mike and I stood watching her go.

"Godspeed." I knelt, picked up a smooth stone, and tossed it into the canyon.

"What does that word mean, anyway? Where does it come from?"

"I'm not sure." I considered his questions. "It sounds better than 'Have a good trip.'"

My ringtone. We had agreed to carry our charged phones with us everywhere around the property, in case there was news to report.

It was Caroline, sounding breathless even though she'd done nothing more vigorous in the last five minutes than apply her brakes. I put her on speakerphone.

"I'm less than a mile away, but I had to call. A car was parked on our road. It had to have been there for at least half an hour, because the lights had gone off."

My heart began to pound in my chest.

"I saw it when my car activated the light. I just got a glimpse of it—a black car."

"Anything more?" Mike pressed her for details. "Make, model, license plate?"

"A car, okay?" Caroline's voice always got shrill when she was flustered. "Black. Not a truck. Not an SUV. A . . . a sedan!" She produced the word triumphantly.

In my mind, I saw an inebriated Boyd Harris falling out of a black sedan.

"Do you think it's still there?" Mike shifted his weight as if preparing to leap into action.

"No. It was parked pointing downhill, so it could leave quickly if it had to. It followed me down, but when I went south on Laurel Canyon Boulevard, it went north."

"Where was it parked exactly?" Mike asked.

"On the big pullout above Stefan's house."

"Thanks for letting us know," I said. "Now go carry out your mission."

Mike frowned as I hung up. "Hard to know if that was him. But we'd better round up the wagons again tonight. And be on double alert from now on."

That night, no one slept well. Maybe it was the full moon that brought all the canyon's creatures out to play, but whatever the reason, we were woken throughout the night by blazing lights. Each time, Mike went to investigate and came back shaking his head.

The first time, "Raccoons." Then, "A stray cat." He grumbled to himself about adjusting the settings so that small animals wouldn't trigger the lights.

"A cat?" I stared at him in dismay. "Did you try to catch it?" Escaped household pets rarely survived in the canyons.

"It was too far away."

We both grimaced, and I returned to my sofa, trying not to picture the cat being hunted down by hungry coyotes. Mike eased down onto his mattress next to me radiating so much tense energy I could see it in the hard set of his neck and jaw.

I let my hand drop down from the sofa.

He took my hand, and we lay that way while I fought an overwhelming urge to run my hands through his short-cropped hair and kiss the back of his neck.

"Good night." I slipped my hand from his and turned away from him before falling into sleep.

Chapter 27

The next morning after breakfast, I pulled Mike aside. "Do you think I'm safe in the studio?" Today, I longed for the soothing rhythm of my potter's wheel, the feeling of cool clay slipping beneath my fingers. Not to mention that I was so behind on my deadlines I didn't think I would ever catch up. My work schedule had been thrown off—badly—the last few days.

"Go ahead. I'm gonna be at the Beast. Anyone who wants in has to go past me."

"Great! Stefan just called. Sometime today—not sure when—he's bringing me Wolfgang."

"Okay, I'll let them in."

I rushed off to my studio, eager to get going. I would be glazing. I wanted to ask Daniela for her help—she loved glazing and was good at it—but feared Viviana would get pissy about it. It bugged me how Viviana would put her hand on Daniela's arm to keep her quiet, as if the girl were a puppet, and how she openly discouraged Daniela from spending time with me.

The thing was I really needed Daniela's help today. But, as the girl's mother, Viviana got the final word. I went off to the pottery studio alone. Within a few minutes, though, Daniela had followed me out.

"Does your mom know you're here?" I asked before I could stop myself.

"She's napping." Daniela gave a little giggle, and we exchanged a glance, hers impish and mine guilty.

"Well, I could use an extra hand. I guess your mom wouldn't mind if you stayed out here awhile." Incredible that I had to feel like this, given the way I was putting out myself and my family to help this woman. I allowed myself to indulge in a fantasy. At the end of all this, we would put Boyd Harris behind bars. Justin and Daniela would go to the colleges of their choice. Viviana would commute two hours a day to a sixty-hour-a-week job, while I made my sculptures and took care of the baby. It was deeply satisfying.

I held up a brush. "Do you want to help me glaze?"

"Yes!"

"You can pick the colors for this one." I handed her a simple vase.

She bit her lip as she pored over the display of wall tiles showing my various color samples. She chose cream and gold glazes and set about her painting. We worked side by side for an hour, sometimes chatting and sometimes companionably silent.

"You're lucky you haven't had any morning sickness," I told her. "I had it so bad with Justin."

"I haven't had any problems at all," she said. "Mom says I've had one of those easy pregnancies. So far, anyway. At least I've got a bump now for sure." She gave me a radiant smile as she patted the front of her T-shirt.

She seemed completely at peace with this huge, unexpected development in her life.

"What's your due date?"

Her brow crinkled. "Due date?"

"What date will the baby arrive?"

She shook her head. "I guess I'll find out when Mom takes me to the doctor."

"Didn't Heather take you to Planned Parenthood?" This, like final exams, must be another thing I'd lost track of. Fortunately, Daniela had only been with us a little more than three weeks and she'd been very early in her pregnancy when she came to us.

Daniela's voice was earnest. She leaned forward, as if it was important to for me to understand. "Mom's here now. She checks my blood pressure and stuff. She doesn't want to waste time and money on appointments for things she can do herself."

I told myself it was okay for Viviana to deal with certain medical matters by herself, simple things at least. I reminded myself that Daniela was her mother's responsibility now, not mine. Which meant that my grandchild was too. It hurt to think of it.

The door opened and Viviana appeared in the doorway, her fierce expression making her even scarier than usual.

I involuntarily jumped a little, then blurted, "Good morning!"

She somehow managed to look elegant and pulled together in an outfit improvised from a pair of Daniela's jeans and one of my T-shirts. I happened to know she wore a bra of Daniela's, and her panties came from an unopened three-pack of inexpensive cotton briefs I'd gifted her from my underwear drawer.

Her eyes moved around the studio, taking in the dust, the clutter, the piles, the overfull trash cans. "Daniela, come with me," she said. "You mustn't bother Nicole when she needs to clean her studio."

"She's actually a big help," I said, meaning it. Next to Daniela stood the vases that she'd glazed since she came in.

"You are very gracious," Viviana said. "Daniela!" She made a tiny, impatient head jerk toward the door.

"I'm not finished with this one." Daniela turned to me for support, which seemed to enrage Viviana. Her voice shrilled and her hair seemed to crackle with electricity.

"You will come with me. Immediately!"

Daniela flung down the paintbrush as if it had burned her hands. She rushed from the studio before I could say a word. I stared at Viviana, who collected herself and smoothed her hair. "You must forgive us. It has been very difficult for us lately."

I couldn't reply at first. It made me desperate to think of the baby. That precious little person, my grandchild, destined to grow up in the same sphere as Boyd and Viviana Harris. I wanted them both at the bottom of the ocean.

"Daniela's a lovely girl," I said. "She's a pleasure to have."

Viviana's mouth twisted. "Then," she said slowly, as if in pain, "she may continue to stay here? With you?"

Astonished, I asked, "What do you mean?"

"I must return to my husband. Soon." There wasn't a trace of drama or self-pity in her. "If I am with him, he will leave Daniela alone."

"If you're with him, he'll hurt you!"

"People do not understand my husband. He loves me."

"He's dangerous."

"We understand each other." She spoke patiently, as if trying to explain something to a small child.

"This will just keep happening. He'll beat you, and you'll come here. And eventually he will come for Daniela." I thought I would suffocate as the nightmare implications of all this started to fully sink in. Being mired in the cycle of violence that threatened the Harris household. Always fearing for our safety. Unable to cut ourselves off from them, because we shared a child. There was no way out.

"It is decided. I will stay tonight and leave tomorrow." Viviana slipped out the door, leaving me alone.

I glazed pots for another two hours, trying to push myself to work faster and more efficiently. I needed to send out as many as possible; lucky for me, my stores were willing to take on the extra merchandise and, so far, had been able to sell it.

But I wasn't supporting just myself and my son anymore. I needed to do the impossible, to work less and earn more.

An idea, like a bee, buzzed its way into my brain. My eyes followed it around. What had Daniela said that time? About Dr. Azirian and her machine?

On a shelf nearby stood a dozen finished vases that had come out of the kiln earlier. They were almost cool.

I had to admire them. The colors were so beautiful, smoky and iridescent purples, golds, greens, and blues. Nobody had glazes like I did.

The idea became clear to me like a deep-sea treasure being slowly pulled to the surface.

I could sell them. I could sell the glazes to other potters and ceramics artists. The glazes would supply some income, maybe enough to take the pressure off me to produce for Clayworks. Maybe enough to carve out some time for the making of art.

My muscles acting ahead of my brain, I found myself picking up the phone and calling Dick Ramsey, one of the biggest ceramics supply dealers in LA. I bought all my clay and most of my tools and other supplies from him.

"Hey, Dick," I asked. "If I sent over some of my glazes, do you think you could sell them?"

A beat. Then, "Maybe."

I told myself not to be discouraged. Dick was kind of a one-syllable guy, not the type to turn cartwheels.

"So, shall we try a few?" I drew up my courage. "Maybe a dozen each of the white, blue, yellow, and red? And a couple of every other color?"

Another beat. "Send 'em over, and I'll give 'em a shot. On consignment."

"Okay. Thanks, Dick." I didn't expect much, but I had to try.

Chapter 28

That afternoon, Justin stormed into the house, cell phone in hand. "Our grades are in," he rasped at Daniela. "Hope you did better 'n me, 'cause I'm fucked."

"Omigod, where's my phone?" Daniela pawed through the backpack on the floor beside her.

His face was . . . not my son's. He was wearing the Man Band again, making his hair stick out funny. His eyes were red-rimmed and underlined by dark circles. He kept licking his badly chapped lips. "I'm going out to shoot some hoops with Mike. Check your email, Mom. Try not to hurl when you see my grades." He disappeared.

It couldn't be that bad. Justin never got anything but As. If I hadn't given birth to him myself and known for sure that Brady was the father, I would never have believed Justin was our child. How could a flunk-out father and a test-taking-impaired mother create an exceptional student? Well, it had happened.

I reluctantly scrolled through my email. There it was, from Laurelmont High. Hoping for good grades despite Justin's warning, I opened it.

One A and three Bs.

As a student, I would have been thrilled with this report card. Wow, an A! But Justin was in a different league. He hadn't had anything below an A since middle school, and now this. These were the most important grades, the last ones seen by the colleges before they made their decisions.

I'd learned enough about the rarified world of Ivy League colleges to know that the three Bs really were a problem, putting a big dent in Justin's hopes for admissions. He must be sick about this.

I looked up to see Daniela watching me. "How'd it go?" I asked her.

She beamed. "Same as usual."

"Good." I assumed that her "usual" grades were good ones, since Daniela was on the honor roll. I was glad for her. I wished I could be glad for my boy. "I'm going to take some water out to the guys."

As Daniela went back to her book, I trekked through the yard toward the car park and the sounds of men in motion. Grunts, the skidding of sneakers, the pounding of the basketball, shouts—it all had an intensity to it that made me pick up my pace.

I burst through the side gate to see Justin playing with a ferocity that had nothing to do with a simple one-on-one basketball game. With all the strength in his thin body, he was running into Mike, stepping on his feet, pushing, grabbing his arms. Justin was playing for his youth, his freedom, his future, all the things he thought were lost forever. He was playing out his rage, his desire to strike back.

Mike, who could have thrown Justin to the ground in a split second, was instead quietly sidestepping him, blocking flying fists, letting him run and dribble the ball, all the while wearing him down. I could see Justin getting more and more tired, while Mike saved his strength. As he allowed Justin to bound past him and shoot, he threw me a philosophical look that said something like, *He'll be okay. Give him time.*

At that moment, I realized something about myself and about Mike. I'd always thought of myself as a brave single mother, soldiering forth all on my own. But it wasn't entirely true. Mike had been there so often, giving his time and attention to my son. He'd listened and helped me make hard decisions. He'd always been a father to my boy. And a partner to me.

Something crumbled and cracked inside me, and I felt this expansion that filled my chest and straightened my spine. Scary thoughts entered my head, and I quickly threw them into a box and shut it, but not before I'd absorbed them into my consciousness. Thoughts like, *I totally love this man*, and *I can't live another second without him.* I shoved the closed box over into a corner of my mind and tried to ignore it, but it jumped around as if something inside it were alive.

I held up two water bottles, which were all the guys needed to stop playing. Justin strode over to me and took a bottle. "D'you see those grades?" he snarled. "Awesome, huh?" He upended the plastic bottle, took a long drink, emptied the rest onto his head, then hurled it into the canyon.

I gasped. "Justin!" If he'd sprouted a tail before my eyes, I couldn't have been more shocked. My son had just sent a foul man-made object out into nature that would pollute the environment for the next four hundred and fifty years.

All the fear, doubt, and frustration of the recent weeks seemed to gather inside me into a single ball of rage. "What on earth are you doing?"

"What does it matter, Mom? What does anything matter?"

"Go get it!"

"What?" Justin emitted a nervous, high-pitched laugh.

"No son of mine just gives up. Now go!" I pointed toward the steep hillside.

Justin looked to Mike for support. He shrugged as if to say, *Can't help you.*

Mike got some cold beers from the house. He and I drank them at the table by the car park while Justin searched for plastic bottles in the hot sun. It would have taken my boy a lot longer if I'd insisted on his finding the exact one he'd thrown.

He came back with a counteroffer: three different plastic bottles in exchange for the one. "Not only have I fixed my mistake," Justin argued, "but I've actually improved the ecology of the hillside." He collapsed into a chair beside us.

"Congratulations! You just made the world a better place." I poured some of my beer into a cup and handed it to him.

Justin drank, then stared bleakly out over the canyon. "What'm I gonna do, Mom?"

"You're gonna keep putting one foot in front of the other. You're gonna do the right thing every single day." Seeing he'd drunk his two inches of beer, I handed him a fresh water bottle.

"But, college, Mom! No way will I get into Princeton now."

"You don't know that. And even if Princeton is dumb enough to turn you down, you're still the same smart, talented boy. You *will* get into a good college, and you'll do well in life."

We sat there for a long moment, listening to the silence of the early evening. Justin leaned forward, fidgeting, his elbows on his knees, one hand loosely holding the bottle. He expelled a deep sigh.

My eyes met Mike's in a look of mutual helplessness. Justin was going to be a father, and there was nothing we could do about it.

So many near misses in life, so many times when we sidestep the consequences of our mistakes through sheer dumb luck.

But this time, the arrow of misfortune had hit its mark. I would have borne this burden for him in a minute, if I could have.

My ringtone. It was Daniela, who was up at the house cooking dinner. "I'm sorry, Nicole. Do we have any Tylenol?"

"I think we're out. But we have aspirin, ibuprofen—"

"Tylenol's the only thing that works for my mom." Her voice dropped, as if she were ashamed to be so demanding.

I suppressed a sigh. Daniela only had a learner's permit and couldn't drive alone. "Okay, we'll send someone down to Johnny's." It was twenty minutes closer than anything else in town.

The three of us considered our options. Justin had promised to help Daniela with dinner. I had to remove pots from my kilns in fifteen minutes, or they would char to a crisp.

"I'll go," Mike said, "if I can borrow your car." He'd left his Jeep at his friend's house in Palm Springs, where he'd picked up the Beast.

He seemed glad to do it; he hadn't left this place for two days and was probably going stir-crazy.

"After I leave, move the Beast over to block the entrance," he instructed me. "Do it right away. I'll be back in half an hour."

"I will," I said, wanting to put out a finger and smooth away the deep lines surrounding his eyes. "Listen, we'll be fine with the entrance blocked off. Stay and have a beer with Johnny if you want."

He hesitated. "Nah."

"No, really. You deserve a break." I didn't need a man to protect me every second of the day. For thirty minutes, with the property closed up, we'd be fine.

"We'll see."

I waved him goodbye and was about to move the Beast when Stefan arrived in his Mercedes to deliver Wolfgang.

"Can't stay—flight to catch!" He called as he extricated Wolfgang from the back seat. The dog knew the drill. After drooling and breathing on me as a friendly form of greeting, he lumbered off to find Midge and Margo in the yard.

I watched Stefan drive away. It was only as I once again turned toward the Beast that it hit me.

I didn't have the key. We'd both forgotten. Mike had taken it with him.

A little sick feeling entered my stomach. *No problem*, I told myself. I reached for my cell to call Mike. I'd ask him to come back right away.

My call went to voice mail. I left him a message, knowing he'd get it soon and come right home.

The sun was beginning to slant in the sky, signaling the start of the long march into nighttime. Viviana's last night with us. Her fourth night away from her violent husband. I wondered how angry he was by now. I thought of Jamie's call. *Assault. Sexual assault.*

No worries, I told myself. We had lights, good locks, and three guard dogs. We would lock the door and windows and call the police if we had to.

I removed my pots from the kiln, quickstepped it back to the house, and gave instructions. Within a few minutes, we were all locked up.

"I'll just feed the dogs and bring them in," I told Justin.

Margo and Midge came running when I called, but Wolfgang was missing. That was unusual. The old dog, no longer active, pretty much lived for his meals these days.

Still, with a sinking heart, I knew what had happened. He had found the open entrance.

Wolfgang occasionally got homesick and had been known to set off by himself down the Trail of Terror, like an elderly gentleman on an afternoon stroll. He was so creaky and out of shape, though, that he never got far. The times I'd gone after him, I'd found him within a quarter of a mile, splayed out in the middle of the road, waiting for someone to come get him.

It was dark now, when the canyon predators came out. Mountain lions were rare, but they did come around, and a single cat could easily take down a basset hound. And coyotes had been known to gang up on dogs his size, particularly the weak and the vulnerable.

My heart sank. We all loved the old dog, with his mournful

face and foul breath. I would die if something happened to him on my watch.

I tried not to think about human predators. "I'll be back in a few minutes," I yelled to Justin. Increasingly worried, I set off down the Trail of Terror.

I half jogged my way around the first two curves, knowing Wolfgang could usually get this far. It was around the third or fourth curve that he typically pooped out. I rounded a bend and, sure enough, there he was, accepting strokes from a man who squatted next to him, checking the tags on his collar.

I stopped as soon as I could, but I was still really close to them.

The man looked up, his dark-blond hair curling around his ears.

I'd seen him before. Darn it. I suddenly realized I'd forgotten my pepper spray.

He gave me a cheerful, open smile. "Did you lose your dog?"

Chapter 29

If it's possible for a human body to go hot, cold, quivering, and utterly still all at the same time, that's what mine did. I wanted to run, but there was nowhere to go, and besides, he had Wolfgang.

I opened my mouth to scream, but only a dry croak came out.

Boyd was watching me with interest. "His tag says he lives down that way." He pointed down the hill toward Stefan's. "I noticed the house number as I drove by."

"Yes, I'll just take him down there now." Had Boyd been drinking? He seemed steady enough. If I could get to Stefan's, I could buzz his housekeeper, Daisy, get in, and call the police. I reached for Wolfgang's collar.

He raised a hand. "Don't bother. I rang the intercom. No one's home there." His tone was pleasant, conversational even, but, all the same, my skin crawled.

Boyd continued to speak, politely, as if he were my table companion at a tea party, and not a trespasser on a remote private road where he had no business being.

"Maybe you can help me," he said. His twinkly-eyed grin sent cold chills down my spine. "I'm looking for an address." And then, reading off a slip of paper from his pocket, he gave me mine.

The sound of my dear, familiar house numbers in this man's mouth made me weak with fear. I shook my head, unable to speak.

He glanced again at the paper, then gave me an appraising look. "Are you Nicole?"

My mouth opened, but nothing came out.

"Maybe I'll see if *Justin's* there." Boyd started up the road, walking fast.

Utter terror at the sound of this man speaking my son's name.

"Wait!" I stumbled after him, calling out to Wolfgang. "Come on, boy!"

The dog trailed behind us. Please, God, where is Mike? He had to be on his way home. In despair, I remembered how I'd pushed him to take his time, have a beer. Have two!

It was almost fully dark. Our new lights would turn on at any moment. I was panting, trying to keep up with Boyd. I called out to him. "What do you want from Nicole and Justin?"

He kept walking.

Panic flooded all my senses. "Justin's a minor! I'm his mother. You have any business with him, you deal with me!" The words came out in a hoarse shriek.

Finally, Boyd stopped walking. He wheeled around, his face hidden by the darkness, but a sly triumph in his voice. "So you *are* Nicole. What a surprise."

I stopped as well. My brain turned in frantic circles. Think. Think of what I could do or say to distract him, slow him down, keep him away from the house until Mike got back.

Something soft touched my ankle. Wolfgang's long, dangling ear. Panting from exertion, he stood nonetheless on full alert beside me. A low growl simmered in his throat, stiffening my spine.

My head began to clear. "How do you have my name?"

"I went to Daniela's school. Talked to her friend Heather, who said I should talk to Daniela's friend Justin."

Heather had given him our address.

"I'm looking for my wife and daughter."

I reached down deep for any strength I could gather. This was my chance.

I faked a little cry of surprise. "Are you Boyd?"

He didn't answer.

"I'm sorry. They left this morning for Las Vegas."

His lip curled. "So sorry I missed them. I'll just see you home."

"Oh, no, I don't need . . ." Dropping all pretense, he grabbed my arm, twisting it and pulling me forward. Boyd's movement triggered the lights, but he barely noticed.

Now I smelled it, the sharp odor of alcohol. I screamed, my puny voice absorbed instantly by the crevices of the canyon. I dug my feet in and tried to twist out of his grasp, but Boyd's hand was like a steel clamp, relentlessly compressing the flesh on my arm, pinching me painfully. With apparent ease, he dragged me the rest of the way up the hill, Wolfgang following on my heels.

At intervals as we walked, the lights blazed to life. I wondered what on earth we had thought we would accomplish by a few lights, except to illuminate the horrors that were about to come.

I tried to somehow send a thought to Justin, as if I could transmit it by air. *Don't let us in. Call the cops.* Over and over I repeated it in my head. *Don't let us in. Call the cops.*

Boyd was dragging me through the car park now. "So they left for Vegas, huh?" He nodded toward Viviana's blue Hyundai, giving me a cruel grin.

We'd reached the yard. Ahead of us, I could see the interior of the living room through the French doors. There was no sign of Daniela or Viviana. Justin stood alone in the living room. He looked up, saw Boyd dragging me through the yard, and reached for his phone, his eyes never leaving us.

Good boy. We just had to hold on until the police got here. Or Mike. In the meantime, I would make things as hard for Boyd as possible.

I took a breath and screamed again at the top of my lungs.

Boyd clamped a hand over my mouth. "Shut up," he hissed in my ear.

Fortunately, the dogs had no such intention. Within the house, Midge and Margo exploded at the appearance of a stranger, howling and leaping against the glass doors. Wolfgang, at my heels, loyally added his mournful bay to the mix of canine voices.

Feeling Boyd's hold on me loosen, I kicked him in the shins. I twisted out of his grasp and ran back the way we'd come. He lunged after me.

"Boyd!"

Both he and I turned at the sound of Viviana's voice. Dressed in her own clothes, with her bag over her shoulder, she stood in the open doorway.

Don't do it, Viviana.

Mike's dogs burst past her and pointed themselves toward Boyd, barking with a frantic urgency.

At that moment, Daniela entered the living room and stopped, gasping at the sight of her mother going to meet her father. Viviana walked toward her husband with a sway in her hips that I'd never seen before.

Boyd looked down at Viviana through narrowed eyes. "Daniela too."

Viviana stopped an inch from her husband and met his gaze, her lips parted. Underneath the controlled calm of her voice lay a tremulous edge of pain. "You have me. I am enough."

Boyd clenched his fist and attempted to step past his wife, but she stood her ground before him. "She must stay here. Please, Boyd!"

That's when it started, a series of events, one leading inevitably to the next, like a row of dominoes falling.

Boyd drew his fist back and punched his wife in the face. She fell to the ground, holding her jaw.

He bounded into the house and straight toward Daniela. Grabbing one of her wrists in each hand, he held her up, smirking.

She kicked him in the kneecap.

He threw her against a wall like a rag doll.

The baby. In an agony of fear, I started to run to Daniela, but Boyd was ahead of me. He grabbed Daniela again and shook her.

"Get off of her!" It was my brave, valiant son coming to the rescue with a baseball bat. He caught Boyd in the shoulder, making a dull thud, but then Boyd and Justin were both grappling for the bat. Justin's face was set in pure determination, but Boyd wrenched it away from him.

Meanwhile, I had gotten to Daniela, terrified for both her and the baby. "Go hide! Now!"

She ran for the kitchen.

Their fight had carried Justin and Boyd near the French doors. The sofa stood between me and them. Desperate, I looked around, my eye falling on my trio of massive candlesticks. My hand closed around the twenty-four-incher.

Justin, facing me, was grabbing for the bat. Boyd, his back to me, raised it against my son.

Moving as if in a dream, I took three running steps forward: on the floor, on the seat of the sofa, on top of the sofa's back.

As I took the third step up and forward, my arms were drawing the candlestick back past my shoulder. At the top of the sofa, I was already swinging it forward with all my strength, as if going for a homerun in the World Series.

Whack! The candlestick connected with Boyd's temple with a sickening crunch as the thing exploded into ceramic shards that flew everywhere. The man emitted a hoarse cry and fell, with me landing on top of him, then leaping up and clawing my way off. I fell to my hands and knees next to him where he lay on the floor, unmoving.

I looked around frantically. What should I do now? Hit him again?

"Nicole." Daniela was kneeling beside me, brandishing scissors and roll of duct tape. She'd known exactly which kitchen drawer they were in.

"You're a genius," I told her.

With Justin's help, working as fast as we could, we pulled Boyd's hands behind his back and taped his wrists together. "Now his ankles. Hurry!" I said as he stirred and groaned.

Grimacing, Justin picked up his feet so that Daniela and I could candy-stripe the tape around his legs from knee to ankle.

He lay there, occasionally moving but, for the most part, inert.

Lying on my side, curled up on the floor as far from Boyd as I could get, I closed my eyes.

My ears rang. My mouth tasted of metal. I had little cuts all over my arms and legs from the broken pieces of candlestick. "Justin," I said.

I must have blacked out for a minute, because now people were talking and moving around me. Mike was kneeling next to me, his voice breaking. "Nic! Are you, okay?"

"Justin!" I tried to sit up.

Mike slipped his hands under my elbows, propping me against the back of the sofa. "Justin's fine. He's talking to the police." His eyes searched my face, my bloodied hands and arms. "We'll get you all fixed up." His face was gray and sagged with horror and regret, making him look ten years older.

I knew what he was thinking. *I wasn't there for her.* I wanted to tell him it was okay. "How's Daniela?"

"Everyone's going to be fine." He looked over to where Boyd was just starting to regain consciousness, groaning and shifting on the floor. "Except for maybe this guy. I didn't know you were Superwoman in your spare time."

"Neither did I."

But I did know. It was just the mama mountain lion, taking care of business.

"You're amazing, Nicole." His gaze warmed me. "I've always thought that, but this? You're incredible!" He reached out and stroked my hair. Around us, the police and paramedics were hard at work. A couple of them cleaned and bandaged our cuts; we had all fallen victim to flying ceramic fragments. An EMT bent over Viviana, who held her head but seemed to be moving around.

As a medic applied a bandage to his arm, Justin was talking to two police officers. "I was fighting with the guy, but then my mom jumped over the sofa and took him out with a candlestick." He pointed to me.

The two officers looked over, curiosity in their eyes. From my spot on the ground, I gave them a little wave.

Justin went on. "We taped his hands and legs together, and then you guys showed up. And Mike."

The two officers grinned at the story. "Good going!"

Had I really done that? The events were swimming together in my mind.

Mike promised to send the police the footage of our struggle, all documented on film. With a huge sigh of relief, we watched as Boyd departed in the back of a police car.

Finally, we were alone in our destroyed home.

"I left you a message," I told Mike. "Did you stop for a beer?"

"No." Mike had never even made it to Johnny's. He'd taken a back road and come upon a woman stranded with a flat tire. "She was alone in the dark." Mike threw up a hand. "I had to stop. She had a spare, but no jack, no flashlight, no tools to speak of. And *you*"—he pointed at me—"don't have any tools in your car, either."

"So what'd you do?" Justin asked.

"I drove her home. Her family'll help her sort out the car. But it took forty-five minutes, so after I dropped her off, I came straight back." Mike's voice broke. His hands shook. He kept looking over at me, his face marked with deep lines.

I'd never seen him like this, so at a loss, so angry with himself.

I tried to tell him it was okay, but my head dropped. My eyes closed.

"Those paramedics gave her something," Justin said.

Mike's voice. "I got her."

He picked me up and carried me out to the door and through the yard to the Beast, where he tucked me into a bed and slipped in beside me, taking me into his arms.

"Sleep," he said. "We're all safe now."

Chapter 30

I woke up, startled, to find sunlight pouring through the open door of the Beast.

After the incredible events of the night before, the last thing I remembered was Mike laying me down on the bed. Sleep had come instantly. Judging by the angle of the sun, it had to be close to noon.

Cautiously, I touched my face and neck, but nothing hurt or seemed to be injured. My arms and legs were bandaged but moved easily under the bedsheet. Hearing voices outside, I sat up.

". . . cops are taking him back to Nevada," Mike was saying. "He's got priors there, so he's going to be in jail for a long time."

"Fine by me," Justin replied.

"Justin!" I called out, struggling up from the bed. Last night, Mike had said he was okay, but I needed to see for myself.

Justin appeared in the doorway, wearing bandages like mine and an expression that told me immediately something was wrong.

I rushed to him. "How are you? Did you get hurt last night?"

"I'm fine, Mom." But his downcast eyes said otherwise.

I looked at Mike, whose face was set in grim lines. He stood on the steps behind Justin.

Daniela and the baby. My voice came out sharper than I intended. "What's going on?" My eyes darted back and forth between their faces.

"This morning, Daniela and Viviana had this huge fight," Justin began. "They went ballistic, screaming at each other in Spanish."

Given the stresses of the last few days, I could see it, especially for Viviana. Picturing Daniela angry, however, was harder to do.

"It was insane, but they finally chilled, and then they left."

I looked around us. We hadn't bothered to close up the car park last night. The blue Hyundai was gone.

"You didn't hear anything, did you?" I asked Mike.

He shook his head, rueful. "Whatever happened, I slept through it."

"Well, okay," I said. "It's odd, but they'll be back eventually." I was thinking about breakfast and the fact that Boyd Harris, for the foreseeable future, had been removed from our lives.

Justin shook his head. "That's the thing, Mom. I went into the bedrooms. They packed up all their stuff and moved out. They're *gone*."

"You're kidding!" With the guys on my heels, I tore across the yard and into the house. In Justin's old bedroom, the few clothes that Daniela had hung in the closet had disappeared. My throat constricted at the sight of that handful of empty hangers.

In my bedroom, Viviana's things were missing as well. In both bedrooms, they had stripped the beds and left the sheets neatly folded on a chair.

Leaving Mike and Justin behind, I ran alone to the kitchen and pulled an antique sugar bowl down from a shelf. Daniela had known we kept emergency cash there, usually about a hundred dollars.

Today, the bowl contained ninety-three dollars. I sighed with relief, ashamed that I might have doubted Daniela for even a second. But how could I not doubt when all the evidence said that she and her mom had run out on us?

Had they at least left a note or a message? I rapidly scanned the kitchen counters and the island, then stopped when I got to the refrigerator.

They had cleared a little place for it among the photos, schedules, and announcements. There, under a Knott's Berry Farm magnet, was a square, cream-colored envelope with foreign-looking handwriting on it. *Nicole,* it said.

I snatched the letter up and ducked into the bathroom, closing and locking the door. I wanted to be alone to receive whatever bad news the letter contained.

In my heart, I knew what it would say. They were going away and taking the baby with them. I would probably never see my grandchild. This little person would grow up under Viviana's care, and who knew? Perhaps Boyd's as well. He, or she, would grow up in fear, feeling trapped, desperate to escape. And I had no say. There was nothing I could do.

My hands shook as I tore open the envelope.

Nicole,

I fear I will not do so well to write this in English. Forgive my mistakes, please.

I write to you because we are both mothers and we understand what mothers must do to protect our children. For our children, we will say or do anything. We will tell lies, play tricks, if it is necessary to keep them safe. As I have had to do, for my Daniela.

So you will understand why it was necessary for us to tell you the story of a baby. In this story, the baby's mother was Daniela, and she was in danger. And we told you that you were the grandmother and asked you to protect Daniela and her child.

And you did so. You saved my daughter from much pain. Perhaps you saved her life. I am very, very grateful.

We did not wish to cause you unhappiness. But it was necessary, and I know that you will understand why.

Someday you will be a grandmother. But it will not be now. And it will not be Daniela's. There is no baby.

All the best to you,

Viviana

I stopped reading and folded the note once, twice, as many times as I could, until it was a small hard cube of paper. My mind was empty, swept clean of thoughts, although I felt the hint of a deluge of emotions just around the corner. And when the deluge came, it would be a doozy.

I stood and walked out to the yard. Mike and Justin were in the pool, hitting around a volleyball—their form of stress relief.

I stood for a minute, watching them. At the moment, the only feeling I would allow myself was happiness for my son. This burden had been too heavy for him, might have broken him had it not been taken away. But, thank goodness, it had. I approached the pool.

"I found a message from Viviana."

They both froze, the volleyball falling into the water, forgotten.

"There's no baby," I said.

They stared at me. "What?"

"There's no baby. There never was."

Chapter 31

After a moment of stunned silence, Justin jumped from the pool in his dripping board shorts and came to me, his face a combination of disbelief and joy. "I don't get it. They just made the baby up? Why?" His forehead creased.

"She needed a safe place for Daniela to stay. She'd heard how I took in Amos for a month and hoped I would do the same for Daniela. But they needed a good reason to give me. So . . ." My voice trembled. "They invented a grandchild for me."

I still couldn't believe there was no baby. No little curly head to kiss. No sweet dimpled fingers.

"That's a crappy thing to do!" Justin commented. "They coulda really messed me up. In fact, they did mess me up." His face cleared. "I guess this means I'm free." As the truth sank in, he spread his arms and began to turn in drunken circles.

"Hell yeah!" His mouth producing a halting beatbox rhythm, he executed a moonwalk—inexpert even to my untrained eyes—around the lawn. Following came hip swivels, head bobs, and various bleats of joy.

Just like that, my boy was back.

Mike hopped out of the pool, water streaming from his body, and came to stand beside me. I thought back over the last four weeks to some of my darkest moments, when I lay in bed praying, *Dear God, please just make this all go away. Please make it a bad dream, something that never happened.*

And now my prayers had been answered in one short letter from Viviana.

That bitch.

The word exploded into my mind.

That evil, conniving so-and-so.

Mike and I stood side by side, watching Justin's antics.

"How could she?" I could barely speak or think. I couldn't feel, either, although I sensed that feelings were about to erupt, one at a time, box by box. "How could she do that to us?"

Mike shook his head, his mind seemingly elsewhere.

"She's a . . . She's a . . ." I couldn't manage to say the words aloud.

She was scheming and duplicitous. An operator, unscrupulous, with the morals of a sidewinder.

And—sorry, but it was true—a shitty mother.

With a shitty little daughter.

That was the worst part of all.

But also so hard to believe. The Daniela I knew—or thought I knew—could not have pulled off a swindle like this.

Once again, I wondered if one could ever really know and trust another person.

"Could she be a pathological liar?" I asked Mike.

Mike, standing next to me, had that same glow that came off him after a good run with the dogs. He was refreshed, vindicated.

"What're you so happy about?" I demanded.

His grin stretched across his face, signaling pure relief. "I knew those condoms worked!"

Now Mike had lost his marbles.

"You're thinking of condoms right now?"

"Yep."

I turned my back on him, filled with self-righteous indignation.

"Seriously," he said. "Do you know how responsible I've felt for this pregnancy? I've been going nuts over it."

"Oh, Mike." I turned back toward him. It should have occurred to me that he would blame himself.

"I never thought it was your fault," I said.

"I did."

My feelings were popping up all over the place now. Oddly unrelated feelings, as if every random emotion that I'd stored up in my life had all been sprung from the same trap. Suspicion, awe, trust, fear, anger.

Love. I looked at Mike, at his dear kind face, his hands, his mouth. I flung myself at him, soaking myself in the process, pinning his arms to his sides, rubbing my cheek on his bare, wet shoulder. "You're such a good person."

"Mom?" Justin stood next to us, panting, red-faced, but wearing an expression of peace that I hadn't seen since the day Daniela arrived.

I took one arm from around Mike and drew Justin into the huddle, making myself wetter still.

"How's it feel?" Mike asked him.

"Fantastic!" Incredibly, Justin was already putting it behind him. Releasing the two of us, he dove back into the pool.

A tiny point of pain was starting between my eyebrows. It pulsed and throbbed, the precursor to a whopper headache. I looked over at Mike, who regarded me somberly. Then he said it, the thing that had been killing me.

"That Daniela, she's one little actress, isn't she?"

She had to be, right? She had lived with us, won us over, been part of our family. Had she been conning us every single day? Every time she put on a big T-shirt to hide her so-called bump, put her hand protectively over her belly, asked me for baby advice, had she been stone-cold lying her face off?

If it was true, her crime was so much worse than Viviana's. Daniela's actions would be a deliberate, minute-by-minute betrayal.

I'd grown to love her, think of her as a daughter. I'd looked forward to sharing the baby with her. I had loved that baby.

Whom I would also have had to share with Boyd and Viviana.

Talk about a recipe for heartache. I was better off without the baby, I told myself firmly, and Justin was much, much better off.

All the stress of the last four weeks, the fear, worry, and anger, the hope and the love, turned into a tangle of emotions that washed over me. I broke into sobs. Big, heaving, tear-spewing sobs.

Mike gathered me in his arms and let me cry against his shoulder.

A familiar grinding sound signaled a car advancing up the Trail of Terror. Mike and I, still standing by the pool, both tensed, then relaxed as we remembered that Boyd was safely behind bars. Justin, oblivious, swam laps.

As the side gate swung open, a pony-tailed, bearded guy appeared. He was so familiar to me and yet so changed I hardly recognized him. Sniffling and wiping away my tears, I stared. It was Grant, Caroline's husband, behind all that hair.

Sure enough, my sister materialized behind him. She ran to me, her joyful smile saying it all. "Nicki! I've got good news!"

I reached out my arms to receive my sister. "So do I."

Chapter 32

Caroline and I declared a draw between our two respective news items: Justin's escape from early fatherhood versus Grant and Caroline renewing their vows.

We had left the guys outside and now sat on her bed, catching up. Caroline looked beautiful, her lips and eyes shimmering, her hair pulled smoothly back into a low knot at the base of her neck. A summery halter top with leggings gave her a cool, pretty look.

She shook her head when I told her about Daniela. "It's so hard to believe." She thought for a moment. "I mean, she was talking about knitting a baby blanket!" Her voice rang with disbelief and contempt. "Yellow, because she didn't know the baby's gender."

"Did you see her do it?"

"No, but maybe she would have eventually." She let out a short laugh. "Anything to keep the lie going." But when she saw my face, the scorn turned to sympathy. "Honey, I'm sorry. I know how fond you were of her. I was too. And the baby."

"It's for the best, I guess." A low gray ceiling of clouds seemed to hang over me when I thought of Daniela.

Caroline's eyes filled with compassion. "You'll have grandchildren. Under better circumstances."

"I know." Years from now. I took a deep breath. "Change of subject. Tell me about you and Grant."

The vow-renewal ceremony would be a brief, touching moment in the midst of a super-fun party with all their friends. There would be tables of food, piñatas hanging from the trees, a series of toasts, and performances by a couple of our musician friends.

Thus, the event would take place in our yard. "I was thinking the third Saturday in June. That's in two and a half weeks," Caroline said. "That's soon, but still gives us time to prepare." She clapped her hands with excitement.

"So," I responded slowly, mentally going over the June calendar, which I had engraved on my brain, "that's two days after my museum opening."

Caroline gasped. "I'm such a horrible sister. I forgot about your opening! Shall we change the date of the party?"

"No," I said, "we might as well not." The truth would come out on the day of the show. I was no good as an artist. I had no ideas, nothing to say. "I'll have something ready in time," I said, hoping it was true. "Whether it's any good, we'll find out. But it'll all be over by the time of your party."

It would be all over, all right.

"You're working on it now? Can I see it?"

I shook my head. "The studio's locked and off limits until the show is over. No exceptions."

"Please? Pretty please?"

But nothing would persuade me. I was too terrified to confide my creative crisis to anyone. Time was flying by, while I just stood there, immobilized.

I couldn't think about it anymore. "How're you and Grant doing? Give me an update."

We settled into chatting position, cross-legged on the bed, facing each other.

"It's as if, when the business failed," Caroline said slowly, "he didn't think he deserved me anymore."

"But what if he loses this new job? Will he leave you again?" My voice came out sharper than I intended it to.

"We won't let that happen. This time, we weren't communicating well. But we've signed up for a couples class called Open and Honest Communication, and we're going to work on that."

"Okay," I said, hoping for the best. "If anybody can make it, it's you two."

Caroline's eyes took on a steely look. "To be honest, the class was only one of my conditions for taking him back."

"One of the conditions?" Now she was talking.

"Another is that I'm going to work. A real job, not just as his office girl. I was thinking of starting an organizing business, and I even have a client lined up." Caroline sounded firm and determined, although I knew she had to be terrified. "I can't just be a hundred percent about him anymore, you know? I need something that's mine."

"Oh, sweetie, that's brilliant!" For my sister, this was a huge step. "Anything else?" I asked. "I hope you're gonna make him shave. And cut his hair."

"That was my first condition."

Justin stuck his head in the door. "You guys gonna stay inside all day?"

"We're coming," I said.

As I walked out into the sunshine, I realized I'd raced off so fast to talk with Caroline that I hadn't yet spoken to my errant brother-in-law. I hadn't seen him since before his meltdown.

I scanned the yard and located my target, who was standing at a distance with Mike overlooking the city view. The two of them were laughing about something. I advanced toward them, picking up speed as I went.

When Grant saw me accelerating in his direction, he dropped his cup. He gave me an apprehensive little wave as I marched up to him.

"Would you give us a minute, please?" I said to Mike.

"Good luck." Mike threw Grant an expression of sympathy and headed off to join Justin in the kitchen.

From the corner of my eye, I saw Caroline emerge from the house, take a pointed look at me standing with Grant, then very deliberately go back inside, leaving us alone. According to the Unspoken Code of Sisterhood, this constituted clear permission from her to speak my mind.

"You got hairy," I said, striving for a jovial tone. His full beard and long ponytail made him seem older and heavier—not a good look.

"Midlife crisis. You know how it is." His voice was doleful.

"No, I don't know how it is. But I do know you broke my sister's heart."

He had the decency to look ashamed. "I've realized my mistake, and I'm back."

"For now."

He stood his ground. "I love Caroline, and she's forgiven me. Can't you do the same?"

I took a few deep breaths to calm myself down and forced myself to speak in a level voice. "Okay, Grant, I do forgive you, because I know Caroline's happy right now." I produced a smile for him, just to prove my sincerity. "And I know you'll be keeping her happy." I gave his shoulder a friendly pat.

He returned a relieved grin.

"Because if you don't, I'll eviscerate you with a pair of garden shears."

The grin vanished, confirming to me that he'd heard me.

I smiled sweetly. "If you'll excuse me, I need to find Mike."

After everything that had happened, I now knew for sure. Mike was the one. All these years he had stood by me, helped me, been my friend. There was no one I trusted more, no one else as good to me.

I found him in the kitchen doing dishes with Justin. "Mike, may I borrow you for a few minutes?"

"Sure." Throwing me a questioning look, he began to dry his hands. "You okay finishing up here?" he asked Justin.

"No problem." My son was already slipping on his headphones for company.

"Thanks, sweetie," I said to Justin as I grabbed Mike's hand.

Half running, I pulled him out the door, across the yard, and through the side gate. I led him up to the Beast. It was locked.

"Open it!"

He unlocked the door and followed me up the metal steps into the Beast's interior.

Alone at last in this cocoon of aqua plastic.

My heart pounding in my throat, I turned to face him and realized I had absolutely no idea of what to say or do next. I stared up at him, pressing his hand between my palms.

Mike looked down at me, his expression combining amusement with the deepest tenderness. And, right under the surface, a desire that made my knees go weak.

And then an ugly little factoid popped out of a dusty, infrequently opened box from my mind.

I hadn't been with a man in eight years.

How did one do these things, anyway? I'd forgotten.

Suddenly paralyzed by shyness, I croaked out a couple of syllables. "I . . . I . . ." Brady's words were coming back to me. *You're cold and unresponsive.* My body went stiff, my hands clammy.

Mike reached out and pulled me toward him, his hand going into my hair. "Nicole." He stroked my hair, while his other arm tightened around me, pressing me against his chest and belly. I took a deep breath of his familiar scent, that blend of pine and peppermint. With my body pressed against his, my legs between his, his arm like a steel band holding me tight, I'd never felt so thoroughly held by a man.

We might have toppled if he hadn't been leaning with his back against a wall for support.

His hand gently tilted my head up. The love and warmth in his eyes told me what I wanted to know. At the same time, his eyes searched my face, maybe looking for the same thing as me, the reassurance that I loved him too. He kissed me then and held me even tighter.

It was as if twenty years had dropped away and we were lovers again, picking up where we'd left off. His right hand slipped inside my blouse and stroked my skin, then moved up to touch my breast while he held me and his tongue played with my lips.

I was back in Santa Monica with that eager, ardent twenty-year-old boy, except now he was bound to me by years of friendship, and he was not a boy, but a man—the sexiest, most exciting man I'd ever met.

I tried to move, but he wasn't having it.

"Hold still," he said, the words not an order but an invitation.

And then he slid his free hand down the front of my pants and inside my panties until he'd reached the end zone. As his fingers began to move oh-so slowly, my knees gave out.

He held me up.

Sweet Jesus Mary Mother of God. I couldn't move, didn't want to move. I'd never felt so loved or so taken care of. Omigod, the way he kissed me with his tongue and he touched me so softly. I clung to him, blissful, drifting on a river of sensation.

It took two minutes.

If that.

My whole body shook, and his fingers continued to move while delicious feelings ran through my body, and I cried out, pushing my face into his chest. And after a minute, he slid down the wall so he was seated on the floor, and I was between his legs, my hip lodged against his erection, which was rock-hard.

I would have to do something about that. In a minute. If movement ever returned to my limbs. A peaceful lethargy lay over me like a heavy blanket.

I didn't know if he'd intended for it to happen, but I knew I would never look at Mike, or think about him, the same way again. We'd been lovers for such a short time that it had seemed like a blip, an aberration compared to the years of platonic friendship between us. But now, in an instant, we'd gone from affection back to passion, from friends to lovers again. And he'd made it so easy for me. I, for one, could never go back, would never want to.

What if it didn't last? What if, after some time, we went our separate ways?

I didn't think we would.

But if we did, it would have been worth it. We would have lived and loved fully and had the experience as a memory. More importantly, we had the present, and the present was everything I could ever want.

Mike continued to hold me tight, his cheek against my hair. I started as the cell phone in his shirt pocket began to vibrate.

"Lemme get rid of this." He pulled out the phone and, without looking at it, laid it down on the floor next to us.

I leaned against him and listened to his heartbeat; then finally, he let me pull away, and our eyes met for a long, scorching moment. And I knew then even more strongly that I loved him, and he loved me, and that we were meant to be together. Finally, I could do it. I could give up all the barriers and the mistrust and the boxes on high shelves and just allow myself to love this man.

"You know I'm not finished with you, right?" Mike said into my ear.

"Good," I replied, showing the sexy, confident woman I'd become. I began to unbutton his shirt, slowly pushing it aside so I could run my hands over his chest.

The cell phone, annoying and insistent, began to vibrate on the floor next to us. I glanced over at it. Even from this distance I could see an emoji with obscenely bright-red lips pursed into a kiss.

What the . . . ? I leaned over and looked more closely, peering until I finally saw the words that sent me spinning—instantly—into turbulent orbit. The message was from someone named Marissa.

"Tonight! Can't wait!"

Chapter 33

My whole body stiffened. My throat closed, and my breath started to come out in angry little puffs.

What an idiot I was.

I sat up, pushing Mike's hand off my thigh. "You have a text." I handed him the phone, squirmed out of his grasp, and jumped to my feet, refusing to look in his direction. My head spun as I stood. My stomach heaved.

I felt, rather than saw, Mike look at the text, then stand up and go to sit on the bench at the Beast's little table. "Nicole," he said.

"I should probably go."

"Hold on!" His voice sharpened. "We've had an agreement for twenty years. Then half an hour ago, you decide to change the rules."

"That's not the point!"

"Then what is?" His eyes questioned me.

"Are you going to cancel this?" I demanded. "Tonight?"

Mike looked startled. "Well, no. I have to see her. I owe her that much."

"You owe her?"

We were on two different planes, unable to connect or understand each other.

"Yeah, I do," he said. "She's a friend." His voice made it sound as if he couldn't believe I expected otherwise.

If he thought he was going to have a relationship with me, while carrying on with these other so-called friends, he could think again.

"How many other girls do you have?"

"Just this one."

Somehow that made it worse.

I wanted everything. His love, his loyalty, his attention. Exclusively.

Maybe it was just too much to ask. From anyone.

"Never mind. Forget it," I said.

"No, seriously." He stood. "Do you really expect me to just drop her without a word?"

His face reflected frustration, annoyance, confusion. No sign of the man who'd been so tender and loving a few minutes before.

And gone was the grown woman I'd become. I was eighteen again and shriveling inside from fears and insecurities.

"Do whatever you want!" I cried, humiliated.

"C'mon, Nicole."

"I don't want anything from you."

His voice roughened. "Don't do this."

"I'm not doing anything." And just like the last time, I ran away and left him behind.

The next morning, Mike texted me.

"Just got a two-week shoot in Mexico--leaving today. Will you take the dogs?"

"Sure," I texted back.

It was Midge and Margo, after all. I would never let them go to some impersonal kennel with cages and inferior food.

"Thx. Tell C I'll be back for her party."

He dropped off the dogs with Justin, not stopping by the studio to tell me goodbye. He was gone, leaving me reeling.

All morning, working at the potter's wheel, my hands formed tortured, lopsided little bowls. In the garden, I took my pain out on the weed population, putting hundreds to death with my Japanese weeding knife. After lunch, I sat on the floor for an hour with my arms around Midge and Margo, letting them lick the tears from my face.

Then I was back in my studio, staring blankly at the three plywood panels leaning against the walls, naked and ignored. It was two weeks to the opening, and I had no concept of what I was going to do. I was in such deep doo-doo that I would never pull myself out, never be able to save myself.

I saw myself, mortified, explaining to the CCMLA board how I'd been really busy, because my son had gotten a girl pregnant, but then she really wasn't, but we thought she was, and her jailbird dad showed up, and I hit him over the head with a candlestick. Maybe they would cut me slack because I was a hero.

No. I didn't think so. *You have two weeks,* I told myself. *Get it in gear!*

Maybe I was just too hung up on the concept of tiles. I couldn't figure out how to make a representation of something in tiles. But what else could I do? I could mold shapes out of clay. How to translate something like that into a flat wall installation?

My eyes fell on the Adopt Me shelf, which bulged with orphans, the hastily piled pieces that no one wanted. I moved over to adjust one particularly precarious grouping, where a sugar bowl sat balanced on a pitcher. As my hand reached for it, the sugar bowl tumbled, the top going one way and the bottom flying the other. I grabbed for both, which sent the pitcher airborne too. For a split second, total silence, while I grasped uselessly at empty air and the pieces of crockery descended. Then, a series of crashes.

After the noise had subsided, I looked at the mess I'd made. The brilliant colors, tangerine and apple green, lay mingled together, interwoven with the white lines of the broken pottery edges. An intact cup handle, separated from its cup, poked up into the air. A portion of the pitcher also stuck out.

I stared at the messy pile of shapes, textures, and colors. It was really kind of beautiful.

Other artists had worked with pieces of broken crockery, but not in the way I was suddenly envisioning. I wondered what it would look like if I added another color, say black. I picked up a black vase—this one rendered homeless by a single unacceptable dimple in its finish.

"We're doing this for art," I said to the vase and pitched it against the wall. The shiny, black remnants with their broken white edges lay among the green and tangerine pieces in an arrangement that could only have been produced by serendipity. I would have had to work for hours to create on purpose such authentically shocking and casual destruction.

I spent a half hour taking detailed, close-up photos of the arrangements of the broken remnants, the way they fit, or didn't fit, with each other as they had come to rest after their fall. Moving automatically, I got a dustpan and swept as many of the pieces as I could into it. Then, instead of throwing them in the trash, I carried them over to the three panels for my mural. I did this twice more, until I'd moved all the pottery remnants to my new workspace. There, I would rely on the photos to reassemble the broken pieces just as they had fallen.

My mind, previously bereft of ideas, now burst open with them. Optimism replaced despair. I would have to paint the panels first. I would need to break more pottery, certainly the entire Adopt Me shelf, plus make some more pieces if I decided I needed particular colors. The two weeks I had left now seemed workable, because now, praise whatever merciful higher power there was up in heaven, I knew what I was going to do.

My moods these days vacillated; later that day, after my morning high in my studio and an afternoon of constructive pottery-breaking, I plunged back into despair over Mike. Seeking validation, I went over to Jamie's and updated her on everything.

"It's about what I would expect from you two," she said, speaking easily, even though we were on another one of her jogs. We were running at twilight in her quiet residential neighborhood, with its mixture of apartment and condo buildings, as well as small houses.

Gazelle-like, Jamie bounded over tree roots and uneven patches of sidewalk, talking all the while. Stoic and suffering, I stumbled along behind her.

I was just able to gasp out a response. "What do you mean, expect from us?" Exhausted, I contemplated taking a page from Wolfgang's book and lying down in the middle of the street.

"You know. Another chapter from the ongoing saga, *Tales of the Emotionally Stunted.*"

Her words stung. "Takes one to know one," I fired back. Jamie had literally not been in love since the twentieth century.

"Exactly! I'm uniquely qualified to judge you objectively and accurately. I mean, he asked you what you wanted. Why didn't you tell him?" She jumped to smack a low-hanging tree branch with her hand.

I silently cheered as she turned us onto a street that would take us back to her home. "Because I can't." I gasped for breath as I talked. "I don't think he wants to give up that other girl."

"What if he does?" Jamie had finally slowed to a walk.

That prospect was almost as scary as the first.

We came to a stop in front of her little white house with red shutters and palm trees. A true friend, Jamie bravely took my sweaty face in her hands and looked directly into my eyes. "This is your window of opportunity. You want him? Tell him how you feel. The minute he gets back."

She dropped her hands and wiped them on her shorts.

I couldn't do that. "What if he doesn't want me?" I wailed. What if I had forever blown it with him? I thought of his steadiness, his goodness to me, and how wonderful he was to Justin. And I thought of our encounter in the trailer, when he had taken me apart and put me back together in a single passionate moment.

How much did he like this Marissa? From her name alone, I could tell she was large-breasted and beautiful. He had gone to her that night, I was sure of it. He had said he would.

"If he doesn't want you," Jamie said, "then you'll know you tried. You'll know you didn't miss out on something good just because you were too scared to go for it."

It seemed like small consolation to me.

As if things weren't bad enough, when I got back to my cell phone, I saw that a text had come in from an unfamiliar phone number. I read it once, then read it again.

"Nicole, I am in Los Angeles, and I must talk with you. Please do me this favor. —Viviana."

Chapter 34

Caroline revolved slowly before me in a peach shift with a sweetheart neckline. Our large fitting room at Anita's Fine Fashions bulged with colorful dresses hanging from hooks on the wall. "Aren't you at least curious?" she asked.

"Nope." I pushed away a tulle skirt that hung over my shoulder and shifted position on the padded seat they'd provided. "I have no need to speak to that woman ever again."

Caroline cocked her head to the side, regarding herself in the three-part mirror. "What about this one?"

"It's too pale for your coloring. If you want to wear peach, try this." I pointed to a different dress, deeper and more vibrant in hue.

"I dunno." Caroline sighed. "I think I really want something more like a wedding gown, except not really a wedding gown. Is that dumb?"

"No. You should have whatever you want."

Anita's was a dress store that also had a large wedding department. We'd asked to try the regular dresses, but I'd seen Caroline glancing over covetously at the area filled with lustrous, beaded white gowns.

"Gimme a minute," I said and went off in search of the sales lady. Seeing her look down at my hands, I plunged them into my pockets. She didn't need to see my paint-and-glue-spotted hands, nicked and scraped from fitting together pieces of broken pottery.

"Would you mind taking these dresses out of our room? I'd like to find her something myself if that's okay. From the wedding selection."

Her name tag said Yvonne. Her bored expression said, *Is it lunchtime yet?* "Fine with me," she said. She pointed me in the direction of a long hallway lined with racks of wedding dresses. They seemed to start with the most expensive and move downward in price.

I zipped by the top-of-the-line dresses—the ones encrusted with pearls, sequins, and beads, festooned with ruffles and frills, dresses with enormous puffy sleeves and ten-foot trains. They were just right if you wanted to look like a float in the Rose Parade.

As prices dropped so did the number of ruffles and pearls, although not as much as I would have hoped. Halfway along, something caught my eye.

A low-necked, off-the-shoulder gown with a gently flaring mermaid-style skirt, in a rich cream silk that had, for the most part, escaped embellishment.

My breathing stopped. So beautiful. So perfect. But not for Caroline.

For me.

Mike would go crazy for me in that dress. But I had to face facts—it wasn't going to happen.

Focus. My sister. A dress for my sister.

Caroline liked striking, unusual dresses. She liked quirky and fashionable. I moved on.

Finally, toward the end of the hallway, I found a few possibles. A cream-colored silk slip dress with fringe, a tea-length chiffon in eggshell white, and a vintage, flapper-style white with silvery beads.

I found Caroline pacing the fitting room in her bra and underwear. "Your phone's been ringing." Her guilty but agitated expression told me she had dug into my purse for an unauthorized peek and was dying to tell me what she'd seen.

"All right, who was it?" We always checked each other's phones even though we'd promised each other we wouldn't.

I tried to ignore the little thread of hope I felt.

"Viviana! She left more messages. It seems really important."

A pang of disappointment, which I pushed away. "Later. Look what I've got for you."

She fell upon my offerings and in fifteen minutes had chosen the flapper dress. It turned out she already had a pair of silver 1920s-era heels that were perfect for it.

"I'm so happy! Thanks! Best sister ever!" She hugged me.

I hugged her back, then cringed as my phone began to ring again.

Caroline, Jamie, and I sat at the kitchen counter tying Jordan almonds into little net bags. They were party favors that Caroline had insisted upon. Jamie and I exchanged a glance of mutual resignation, then set about our chore without complaint. As Caroline's sister, I was fated to tie little bows until I toppled. Jamie, I had roped in with offers of home-cooked meals.

"Look at your hands," Jamie said to me, eyeing my reddened skin, broken nails, and numerous cuts and scrapes.

"Occupational hazard. I just need to moisturize."

I was working late every night. *You should just be glad of that,* I told myself. My sister and son were back on track. I was making art. I couldn't complain just because I'd lost the man I loved.

Jamie and Caroline both thought I should return Viviana's calls. "What if it's important?" Caroline asked.

"It's important to her, not to me."

"And another thing," Jamie said. "Do you plan to follow my advice? Tell that gorgeous hunk that you want him?"

"He's not going to give up this other woman. He straight out told me so."

Caroline put down her candy scoop. "I don't believe that. What did he say?"

I tried to remember.

"I need his *exact words.*" Bits of candy and netting lying forgotten around her, Caroline focused her full attention in on my issue.

"After he and I . . . got together, he had this date he'd made with a girl named Marissa. And I asked if he still planned to go. And he said yes, that she was a friend and he owed her, that he couldn't just drop her without a word." Flustered, I tried to give her a *See, I told you so* look, but for some reason, the words didn't sound quite the same to me now as they had the other day.

They stared at me, faces skeptical.

"You're an idiot." Being a friend, Jamie said it in a loving way.

Caroline began to talk her way through her thoughts. "I think he was saying he owed her an explanation . . . because he was going to break up with her."

"He . . ." My brain felt slow and tired. "What? Break up with her?"

Caroline's face now glowed with certainty. "Exactly. He needed to see her so he could break up with her in person. 'Cause he's a good guy."

"Oh," I said in a tiny voice.

Were they right? Had I really blown it that badly?

Chapter 35

Finally, a call I *wanted* to receive. It was Dick Ramsey, with a surprise reorder on my glazes.

My insides went liquid, while my mind churned. "You've already sold what I sent you?"

"In a day and a half. When people heard Clayworks was starting to sell its glazes, they lined up. I've just been too tied up to get back to you with another order."

It was more words than I'd ever heard him string together in all the time I'd known him.

"That's wonderful! So you want the same number—a dozen of each . . . ?"

"I'll take a hundred each of the white, blue, yellow, and red, and fifty each of every other color."

I was sure I'd misheard. *"A hundred!"*

"I have a mail-order business. I'm going to do an insert in my next catalog."

My mind raced through all the practical considerations. "I . . . I'll . . . have to check how much I've got in stock." My voice came out high and squeaky.

I already knew the answer, though. My manufacturer, Ramirez Brothers, was a family business that usually made me up glazes in small lots, a dozen at most. I managed to lower my voice to the acceptable range. "My glazes are hand-made in small amounts by . . . artisans, with . . . all-natural ingredients," I told Dick, my heart fluttering in my chest like a flock of birds. "We may have to . . . position them as specialty glazes at . . . higher prices."

My head spinning, I placed a few more calls. Good thing Chico Ramirez had a lot of brothers, not to mention all his cousins and in-laws. He was also a can-do sort of guy, assuring me he could keep the quality up while delivering the amounts Dick wanted. Dick was sure he could sell as much glaze as I could give him.

I negotiated quantities and prices with the two of them and signed off, Dick's final words like the sweet sound of a ringing cash register in my ears. "I'll also talk to some of my affiliates around the country. I think they'll be interested."

I tried to force down my soaring hopes, but I couldn't help it. I could see it. If this worked, my glazes would put Justin through college and maybe pay some of the other bills as well. I could slow down the assembly line of vases and dinner sets. I would have time to do what I'd dreamed of, or at least try for it. I would become a ceramics artist.

The week before the opening, I worked night and day on my mural, thrilled to have finally found my direction and grateful to have something time-consuming to take my mind off Mike.

I was due to install the piece today at 2:00 p.m. at CCMLA. The invitation-only opening was tomorrow night, and the show opened to the public the day after. I might bomb completely, but at least I'd have something to show. If people hated it, I would give myself the time-honored label of "controversial." It was old, and it was tired, but it could still offer some solace to a struggling artist.

Stefan's work supervisor had come with his pickup truck and, puffing and gasping, helped me load the three massive wrapped panels into the back. "I can take it from here," I told him. "The museum staff will help me unload and install these. I'll bring the truck back to Stefan later on."

Waving away Diego's protests, I drove off in a combination of relief and terror. Tomorrow night, it would all be over. I hoped my piece would get a good reception. Realistically, I would probably never make a living as a pure artist; there wasn't a large market for twelve-by-nine-foot ceramic walls. But I wanted the respect.

The people at CCMLA greeted me warmly and, to my relief, had no difficulties installing the three panels on the wall. For the first time, I saw all three joined and hanging together as a single assembled piece. We all stood there, taking it in—me, the museum director, a fair number of the board members, including Miriam Fletcher, and the workmen.

My breath caught. For the first time, I appreciated the chance these people had taken on me. My piece was not only huge, but also right at the entrance—the first thing you saw when you entered the exhibit. If it didn't impress, some people might turn away at the door.

But it did impress. I thought so, at least.

It looked incredible. The left side and bottom third of the mural showed a hillside covered in an avalanche of broken pottery beyond saving, objects that had been destroyed by carelessness, mistreatment, or neglect. The bottom of the painting seemed almost to give off a smell of putrefaction; the dark pieces had been crushed and pulverized to the point where almost nothing could be reclaimed. But as your eye moved upward, the darkness gave way slowly to bits of color and texture, then to more and more of it. Finally, surging upward through the crockery were vertical strips of green, some still below the surface and others that had emerged blooming into the blue sky and sun at the top of the highest panel, also rendered in ceramics.

Miriam Fletcher sidled over to me. "And how is this a paradigm for how we live?"

"It just feels that way to me," I said. "Things fall apart and come back together. Everything can be completely broken around you, and then life starts—very slowly—to reassert itself."

"I assume you know that the use of broken ceramics in artwork is not new," she ventured.

I was ready for her. "True, and if you're referring to Julian Schnabel, I'm well aware of his work. Mine is very different in theme and in the way I use the materials. Still, I gave him a nod in this piece." I pointed out the lower left corner of my piece, which contained three shards of pottery with virtually the identical shape and color as those in the lower left corner of a famous Schnabel piece.

"Interesting!" she said. The other board members swarmed in to congratulate me—and her, for having found me.

Miriam's relief was almost tangible. "You did it! Thank you, Nicole. Let me introduce you to some people from the local media. They're doing pre-opening reviews." And she bustled me off to do publicity for our fabulous museum show, and for my place in it.

At the opening, I tied up my hair and wore a beaded tea-length dress and stood back collecting compliments from the CCMLA board and reviewers from the LA and San Francisco papers. I was introduced to moneyed, high-influence investors and bloggers, who asked what I was making next and did I have time to give an interview?

My piece was a standout; I choked up every time I looked at it. So much worry and thought had gone in to whether others would like it or not. I was glad they did, but most of all, I was glad that I liked it.

I was proud of myself. And sad.

Because Mike wasn't there. Twice during the evening, I had jumped, convinced I'd caught a glimpse of him somewhere in the crowd. It was silly of me. He had sent me a text to wish me luck and say he was sorry to miss the opening; he was stuck on this shoot in Mexico. But he would be at Caroline's party.

I had kicked ass at my museum opening. I should be happy about that, and I was. I reminded myself of other good things, that Caroline and Justin were happy again. Caroline had chosen to continue living with me until her ceremony. "I'll move back in with Grant afterward. That'll make it extra special."

I was grateful to have her. And to have Justin, who was seeing friends again and seemingly unscarred by the Daniela episode. I had found myself talking to him about it one morning as he headed into the shower. He stood in the hallway holding his towel and hairbrush.

"I know it was a lousy thing for them to do," he said. "But, if it saved Daniela from getting beaten up and hurt, I don't mind it so much."

"Really? You were so unhappy."

"I know, but not for long, and it all went away. Meanwhile, that guy could've killed Daniela."

I shook my head.

"Mom, I'm fine."

"What about your grades?"

His eyes went sober. "That was my fault. Nobody made me screw up my grades except me." He shrugged. "I'll just have to deal with it." He headed into the bathroom. Behind the closed door, I heard the water start.

He had forgiven and moved on. I swelled with pride. My boy had grown up.

Or maybe not entirely. Happy now, he was beatboxing in the shower. *The* noises made their way through the bathroom door.

I stood, listening, so relieved to see him back to his old self.

Forcing my voice to sound normal, I yelled, "I'm going out to the studio!"

"Go in peace!" he yelled back.

As I left the house, he was changing to a falsetto for a new song. "*So much, baby, that I want to say . . .*"

Thank goodness, my son was okay and on the right track, despite Viviana's inexcusable behavior.

Although Justin seemed to have excused it. But could I?

What if it had been the other way around? Would I have been willing to play a despicable trick to save Justin from injury, maybe even death?

I had thought I'd do anything to protect my son. I would certainly give my life for him. But it was another thing to invade the lives of strangers and create mayhem for them. We were lucky things had turned out the way they did, that we'd all been okay.

And yet we weren't okay. At least, I wasn't. I was bitter, angry at Viviana for what she'd done. I guessed I didn't have Justin's resilience and generosity of spirit. I grieved for Daniela—the girl I thought would become like a daughter to me—and for my tiny grandchild, who had never existed.

And, although it had nothing to do with Viviana, I had lost Mike, maybe forever. Even becoming an artist wasn't enough to fill that empty hole.

I hadn't realized how much love I had inside me, love that I yearned to give.

Chapter 36

It was the day before Caroline's party and the time I would see Mike again. I'd gone through the motions of helping Caroline rent tables and chairs and hire a caterer, all of which Grant was paying for. In my circles, where large parties relied on potluck dishes and borrowed tables, this was huge, a testament to his enduring love.

I'd bought beverages and even managed to find a great dress, a feminine, swishy floral print. It featured more cleavage than I'd ever shown in my life, but I figured if there had ever been a time for me to flaunt what I had, this was it.

A text came in from Stefan. "So sorry, darling, but may I increase my miniscule plus two to an eensy weensy plus four?" It was no surprise. He tended to have an entourage for most occasions.

"Of course. You don't even need to ask."

"You're too good to me."

"For you, Stefan, anything!" It was one tiny payment, gladly made, against the debt I owed him for his friendship.

I noted the plus four next to his name on the guest list, then scrubbed and tidied the house.

And now, for the fun part: a few hours to primp for tomorrow. I prepared a tray with bowls of face mask and cucumber slices, damp washcloths, manicure supplies, and a tall glass of ice tea, then carried it out to the picnic table.

I had something to celebrate too. I'd gotten a big check from Dick Ramsey, along with an order for more glazes, and a handwritten note: *Can't keep this stuff in stock. Can I get an exclusive arrangement with you? Will call you next week with a proposal.*

An exclusive deal? I'll have to see if his terms are good enough, I thought contentedly. This check, for an amount far more than

I'd expected, was going straight into Justin's college fund. I wished Mike were here so I could tell him about it.

It was a balmy day, made cool by a stray breeze. My hair tied up in a knot, I sat on a nearby chaise lounge, pulled down the neckline of my blouse, and applied my homemade honey/yogurt/oatmeal skin mask. It went on in gritty wet lumps but couldn't be beat for moisturizing and exfoliation.

I coated my face, neck, and shoulders, then sat for a moment, trying to clear my mind. It kept going to Mike. To his steady kindness. His humor.

That moment in the trailer.

Thinking about his hands and his lips, his body, I shifted restlessly on my chaise lounge while lumps of oatmeal fell.

My nails. To capture Mike, I would need perfect nails. Meticulously, I painted all ten of them, settled back onto my chaise, and, taking extra care with my wet polish, managed to transfer a cucumber slice to each eye.

Now I could relax. In fact, I had to. Immobilized by the cucumbers on my eyes, the foam pads between my newly polished toes, my face and shoulders coated in oatmeal, I could do almost nothing except sit still and let it all dry.

The feeling of safety, which I would never again take completely for granted, the warmth of the day, the sweet scent of growing, living flowers, all finally led to contentment. One day, I told myself, I would make a sculpture that captured this feeling. Sighing with pleasure, I stretched my legs out on the lounge in the sun.

"Nicole?"

I lurched up from the chaise, cucumber slices flying.

Viviana looked small and tired, but elegant in a simple pale-green wrap dress and three-inch heels.

Between the oatmeal and the foam, I felt at a distinct disadvantage. I would have grabbed up my stuff and retreated to the house, but I wasn't about to ruin the three coats of Passionate Plum on my fingers and toenails.

Struggling for dignity, I glowered at her. "How dare you come to my home? Leave immediately."

She pulled up a deck chair and sat down next to me. "I will take only a moment. Please. Daniela is very, very angry with me."

"So am I."

"She does not talk to me."

Who could blame her? And did Viviana really think I cared what her problems were? After what she did to my son? And to me?

"It is because of you," Viviana said.

"Me?"

"Yes, Daniela is angry at me, because of you."

I would never have allowed myself to show an interest, but I didn't have to. Viviana was already beginning her story.

"You know I would do anything to save her from Boyd. So I had to . . ." She lowered her eyes and swallowed hard, as if plucking up her courage. "I had to play a trick to her."

I studied my nails, feigning a lack of interest.

"Daniela told me she had been with your son. She said they had used the protection, but she was still afraid."

She paused to take off her sunglasses and wipe them clean, as if stalling for time. "So I had an idea to save my girl. I gave her a pregnancy test, and I told her it was positive."

"And . . . ?" I stared at her, waiting for her to go on.

She said it again, elucidating the words as if talking to a simpleton. "*I told her the test was positive.*"

"You mean . . .?"

Viviana huffed, seemingly unable to fathom that anyone could be so slow. "I am an expert. She is sixteen. She believes what I say."

"So, all that time, she really thought she was pregnant?" I

tried to wrap my brain around it. "But, what about when she got her period?"

"Daniela's periods come only every three or four months. I only needed you to keep her for four weeks, six at the most."

"Oh, was that all?" I could feel my eyes rolling.

"Then I planned to take her to my country, where my family could protect her."

"Is she in Chile now?"

"No, we will stay in Las Vegas after all. Boyd will be in prison a long time, so Daniela is safe. And I will be close to my husband. I will visit him."

Visit her husband. There was apparently no end to what Viviana would do for love.

"Have you stopped to think for even a minute what you did to my son? And to me?"

Viviana pressed her lips into a thin line. "My daughter was in very serious danger. What did your son suffer? A few unhappy moments."

I boiled over. "You put us in danger!" I pointed a finger at her. "Why did you come here today? You hadn't done enough damage already?"

"Because Daniela became very angry when she learned the truth. She says you will think she lied and tried to trick you."

"She's right. I did think that." My red-hot fury at Viviana swirled and mixed with the cooler waters of relief. At least Daniela hadn't lied. She'd been duped too. "Why are you telling me this?"

"So that Daniela will forgive me and allow me into her life again." For the first time, after all we'd been through, Viviana started to cry in my presence. A wet blotch appeared on her pale green dress.

"Why didn't you tell me right up front, in your note?"

She sobbed. "Because she loves you so much. I wanted her for myself. I wanted to keep you two apart. But instead, she wouldn't speak to me. She said she never wanted to see me again."

The wet blotches grew as her tears fell. "I would give my life for her. I want her to love me."

I thought of Daniela hanging out with me in my studio, admiring my work, asking me for advice, while Viviana looked on from a distance with her broken arm.

And then I found my oatmeal-covered self patting the awful woman awkwardly on the shoulder. I knew where she was coming from. With all her heart, Viviana yearned to love and protect her daughter, to be close to her.

"Daniela knows you love her."

"I hope so." Viviana sniffled and blew her nose.

"She knows you're doing the very best you can for her."

"Thank you," she said. "I knew you would understand."

Chapter 37

To learn that Daniela really was the girl I'd been so fond of had given me back some of my faith in people and in myself. The first guests would arrive in about half an hour, and I was ready to party.

And I was going to see Mike. I didn't know what was going to happen, but I'd done all I could to rock his world with my beauty. My hair framed my face in gentle waves. A bit of mascara brought out my eyes, and my glossed lips were pink and kissable. My boobs looked perky in a push-up bra, my belly flat in a pair of Spanx. The last thing I did was put his silver chain around my neck and cross my fingers for luck.

Had he really broken up with Marissa? We would have to see what happened. I wandered out of my bedroom and into the kitchen. Thanks to the caterers, I had little work to do. In a second, I would check on Caroline and help her finish her hair and makeup.

I paused at the open French doors to look out at the yard. Rows of extras flowers, which I'd planted at the last minute, brightened the perimeter at the canyon edge. At one side of the yard, under a shade canopy, stood buffet and dining tables. At the other side were microphones, chairs, and a podium for the ceremony and musical performances. A valet service manned the entrance down at Laurel Canyon Boulevard, handling the tricky job of parking all those cars down below and bringing guests up and down the Trail of Terror by shuttle.

I could sense a great party in the making. Happy for my sister, and for myself, I wandered into the kitchen, which hummed with caterers. "Excuse me." I slid by them to the refrigerator. I just wanted a glass of water.

Caroline had stuck the guest list on the fridge door, probably to have it nearby for last-minute changes. Better take this down before people started to arrive. As I did, my eye fell on a name. Mike's.

Next to Mike's name, in Caroline's handwriting, were the words *Plus one.*

My heart did a loop-de-loop in my chest.

Mike was bringing a date.

On the inside, I was dissolving into a pool of liquid panic. I simply could not face Mike if he was with a date. I would cry, I would throw up, I would die. I would disgrace myself and ruin my sister's party.

On the outside, I remained calm. I tucked Caroline's hair up into a French braid and then, at her request, took it down. "Grant likes it better that way," she said. We put flowers in her hair instead, tiny daisies and baby's breath, and I darkened her eyelashes with my black mascara.

"You look beautiful," I told her.

"So do you."

I couldn't understand why she hadn't warned me, but I knew she had to have thought it was better for me this way. I wouldn't allow myself to bring it up. This was her day, and if I could help it, there was no way I would spoil it for her.

The guests began to arrive. I hugged and kissed and cooed greetings while my peripheral vision scanned for Mike. If I could spot them first and check her out, get my equilibrium back, I might be able to get through this unscathed.

How could he do this to me? How could he hurt me like this?

There was Jamie, who had just walked in. I signaled frantically. "C'mere!" Thank goodness! Reinforcements.

I clutched her arm. "Help me. Mike's bringing a date!"

Her mouth dropped open. "That swine!"

I saw him, gorgeous in a plain black T-shirt and sports jacket. Tears sprang to my eyes. I had blown it so badly with him, and now I'd lost him. I would never find anyone like him. I would be alone for the rest of my life.

"Head high," Jamie whispered. "You look sensational!"

Beside Mike stood the enemy in a coral dress, mainly hidden by the crowd, but visible enough that I was sure I detected a great body. I braced myself to see the woman he loved more than me. The person in front of her stepped aside.

It was not a woman with Mike, but a girl. A girl who, when she saw me, flew across the room toward me with her arms open.

"Nicole!" She flung her arms around my neck. "I'm so sorry. I didn't know. You have to believe me."

"It's okay," I said, joy flooding me. "Your mother told me."

We both spewed tears.

"I've missed you so much!" Daniela said. "I'm living in Vegas again, but could I come visit you this summer? And maybe stay for a while?"

"I'd love that more than anything! But your mom . . . ?"

"She said it was okay." Daniela sniffed, her expression growing cold. "She's still on this big guilt trip."

I knew what it must have cost Viviana to allow something like this. "She loves you," I said as gently as I could. "She's trying to show you that."

I stood in a circle with Caroline, Grant, Justin, Jamie, Daniela, and

Mike. The people I most loved in this world. I didn't dare look in Mike's direction.

"We decided to surprise you!" Caroline was delighted with how she'd pulled it all off. Apparently, Viviana, tired of my rejections, had called my sister, who had allowed her to come by the house yesterday. It had been Caroline's idea to invite Daniela to the party.

Grant pointed to his watch. The ceremony would start soon. "Fifteen minutes." He looked handsome again, clean-shaven, his hair neatly clipped. I was glad to see he was obeying Caroline's instructions.

"It's great you were in LA, so you could come," I said to Daniela.

"She wasn't," Caroline said.

"Mike drove up to Vegas last night to get me." Daniela nodded in his direction.

I finally looked at him. His face wore the same determined lines as in the moment before a dangerous stunt—deadly serious and focused on the job at hand.

He spoke at the same time that I did.

"I have to talk to you."

"We need to talk."

Caroline fluttered her hands at us. "Go."

Grant pointed to his watch. "Thirteen minutes."

"We'll wait for you," Caroline said, serene and completely in charge.

Holding hands, we ran across the yard and through the side gate, looking for privacy. The Beast, with its aqua plastic environment, was gone, as Mike had returned it to his friend in Palm Springs in exchange for his Jeep. We ran on through the car park and down the Trail of Terror, where at last we were alone beneath the overhanging shrubbery.

We stood, facing each other, panting slightly. I was so conscious of him, his nearness, his silver-blue eyes, which glowed fiercely in this moment, as if nothing was going to stop him this time or get in his way.

Don't blow it, I told myself. Just tell him how you feel. It wouldn't be hard to do this time. I wasn't scared anymore of embarrassing myself. The only thing that scared me now was losing him.

Mike took both of my hands in his. "I went to Marissa's to break up with her."

"I know," I said humbly. "Caroline explained it to me."

"It's you, Nic. It's always been you." Mike's voice shook.

"It's always been *you.*" I'd known it but had hidden it from myself in one of my darn boxes.

His expression cleared, his shoulders relaxing. "I love you." He gave me a deep, lingering kiss that replaced all rational thought in my head with a random tumble of emotions. Joy, lust, relief, disbelief. And deep, crazy love.

We loved each other, and our love was everything. It was true friendship and understanding, trust, loyalty. And it was passion, setting me on fire.

Our lips came apart for a moment and we caught our breath, our cheeks touching, his hand on my hair.

And then he got down on one knee and pulled a square velvet box from his coat pocket while my mouth opened in shock.

"Marry me, Nicole?" His face was so open and honest and dear to me.

"Oh my goodness!" It was all I could say.

A crease appeared in his forehead. "Will you? Marry me?"

"Of course I'll marry you!"

He stood and slipped the ring on my finger. I only had time for a brief glance. The ring was fabulous, but I was busy looking into his eyes and crying and kissing him. "I love you so much!"

But then I stopped. "Mike?"

"Mmmm?" His lips were just beside my ear.

"I've been thinking. There's something I want."

"Anything."

"I want a baby."

He pulled away from me, startled. "A baby?"

I nodded. "Why should I wait for a grandchild? I'm thirty-eight. I can have my own baby."

Did I dare say it? I plunged on. "With you, I mean. Our baby."

I held my breath, waiting for his answer.

He gazed down at me, impassive, except for twinkling eyes and a single raised eyebrow. "I'm in."

"Really?"

"Let's make one tonight."

"This is great!" All my dreams were coming true.

"Let's make it now."

"After the party."

I stood with Justin and Daniela, watching as a radiant Caroline renewed her vows of eternal love with her soul mate of twenty-four years and husband of twenty. Afterward, Daniela went to congratulate them, while Mike pulled Justin aside. Taking my arm, he said, "Listen, Justin, I love your mother—a lot. I've asked her to marry me."

Justin lunged backward in mock horror. "And she said yes?"

"Hard to believe, but yeah. She did."

"Well, in that case . . ." Justin shuffled over to me, blushing a little. "If you really want to marry this guy, I can't stop you, I guess." He gave me a hard hug and wiped his eyes.

Then he and Mike hugged, pounding each other on the back a few times.

"No, seriously," Justin said. "It's cool. I'm down for it." More eye-wiping.

All the weeping and hugging were attracting attention. "Let's not tell anyone else right now," I said. "This is Caroline's night."

Too late. She and Grant were bearing down upon us, and a minute later, the news was out.

"I'm so happy for you!" Caroline sniffled delicately into a tissue. "If you want some time with him tonight, we'll be here."

"No. This is *your* night."

"Oh, I'm an old Sadie, Sadie, married lady! And besides, we're not leaving. This party's just getting started."

"What about Justin?"

"He'll be here with us, Nicole! Go be alone with your man."

"I booked a suite at the Four Seasons," Mike said. "Just in case you said yes."

And so it was Mike and I who made the traditional exit of the bride and groom, running across the lawn and out to the car park to drive down the Trail of Terror in his Jeep, while our dearest friends and family held their drinks aloft in a toast—to us.

The End

About the Author

A**ward-winning novelist Anne Pfeffer** grew up in Phoenix, Arizona, where she had a quarter horse named Dolly. After college and living up north, she escaped back to the land of sunshine in Los Angeles. She has worked in banking and as a pro bono attorney, representing abandoned children in adoption and guardianship proceedings. Anne has a daughter living in New York and is the author of four books in the YA/New Adult genres.

Connect with Anne

annepfeffer.com
Twitter.com/AnnePfeffer1
anne@annepfeffer.com

Made in the USA
San Bernardino, CA
07 April 2019